PENGUIN CLASSICS
Maigret's Pickpocket

'Extraordinary masterpieces o...
– John Banville

'A brilliant writer'
– India Knight

'Intense atmosphere and resonant detail . . . make Simenon's fiction remarkably like life'
– Julian Barnes

'A truly wonderful writer . . . marvellously readable – lucid, simple, absolutely in tune with the world he creates'
– Muriel Spark

'Few writers have ever conveyed with such a sure touch, the bleakness of human life'
– A. N. Wilson

'Compelling, remorseless, brilliant'
– John Gray

'A writer of genius, one whose simplicity of language creates indelible images that the florid stylists of our own day can only dream of'
– *Daily Mail*

'The mysteries of the human personality are revealed in all their disconcerting complexity'
– Anita Brookner

'One of the greatest writers of our time'
– *The Sunday Times*

'I love reading Simenon. He makes me think of Chekhov'
– William Faulkner

'One of the great psychological novelists of this century'
– *Independent*

'The greatest of all, the most genuine novelist we have had in literature'
– André Gide

'Simenon ought to be spoken of in the same breath as Camus, Beckett and Kafka'
– *Independent on Sunday*

Georges Simenon was born on 12 February 1903 in Liège, Belgium, and died in 1989 in Lausanne, Switzerland, where he had lived for the latter part of his life. Between 1931 and 1972 he published seventy-five novels and twenty-eight short stories featuring Inspector Maigret.

Simenon always resisted identifying himself with his famous literary character, but acknowledged that they shared an important characteristic:

> My motto, to the extent that I have one, has been noted often enough, and I've always conformed to it. It's the one I've given to old Maigret, who resembles me in certain points . . . 'understand and judge not'.

Penguin is publishing the entire series of Maigret novels.

GEORGES SIMENON

Maigret's Pickpocket

Translated by SIÂN REYNOLDS

PENGUIN BOOKS

PENGUIN CLASSICS

UK | USA | Canada | Ireland | Australia
India | New Zealand | South Africa

Penguin Books is part of the Penguin Random House group of companies
whose addresses can be found at global.penguinrandomhouse.com.

First published in French as *Le Voleur de Maigret* by Presses de la Cité 1967
This translation first published 2019
002

Set in 12.5/15 pt Dante MT Std
Typeset by Jouve (UK), Milton Keynes
Printed and bound in Great Britain by Clays Ltd, Elcograf S.p.A.

ISBN: 978-0-241-30417-4

www.greenpenguin.co.uk

Maigret's Pickpocket

1.

'Sorry, monsieur.'

'Not at all.'

It was at least the third time since the corner of Boulevard Richard-Lenoir that she had lost her balance, bumping into him with her bony shoulder and crushing her string bag full of groceries against his thigh.

She apologized automatically, neither embarrassed nor genuinely sorry, then carried on gazing straight ahead of her with a calm and determined expression.

Maigret took no offence. It was almost as if it amused him to be jostled. That morning, he was in a mood to take everything light-heartedly.

He had had the good fortune to catch an older bus with a rear platform, in itself a source of great satisfaction. These buses were becoming more and more infrequent, since they were gradually being withdrawn from use, and soon he would be obliged to tap out his pipe before being enclosed in one of the huge modern vehicles inside which you feel imprisoned.

The same buses with platforms had been in circulation when he had first arrived in Paris, almost forty years earlier, and in those days he had never tired of taking one along the large shop-lined boulevards on the Madeleine–Bastille line. That had been one of his first discoveries.

That and the café terraces. He had never tired of the terraces either, where you could sit in front of a glass of beer and watch the ever-changing sights of the street.

Another source of wonder in that first year: by the end of February, you could go out without an overcoat. Not every day, but some of the time. And the buds were beginning to swell along certain avenues, especially Boulevard Saint-Germain.

These memories reached him in waves, because this was another year when spring was early, and that morning he had left home without his overcoat. He felt as light as the sparkling air. The colours of the shops, the food stalls, the women's dresses, were all bright and cheerful.

He was not thinking of anything in particular. Just a few disconnected little thoughts. At ten o'clock, his wife would be having her third driving lesson.

This was an unexpected, even amusing turn of events. He could not have said how they had reached the decision. When Maigret was a young police officer, it had been out of the question for them to afford a car. Back then, such a thing was inconceivable. Once the years had gone by, he had never seen the need for one. It was too late to learn to drive. Too many things were going through his head. He wouldn't notice a red light, or would stamp on the brake instead of the accelerator.

But it would be nice, on Sundays, to be able to drive out to Meung-sur-Loire, and their little house there.

They had made their minds up recently, on an impulse. His wife had protested with a laugh:

'You can't mean that . . . Learning to drive, at my age!'

'I'm sure you'll make a very good driver.'

And now she was on her third lesson and as nervous as a girl about to sit the baccalauréat.

'How did it go?'

'The instructor is very patient.'

The woman standing next to him on the bus presumably couldn't drive. So why had she gone to do her food shopping on Boulevard Voltaire, when she must live in a different neighbourhood? One of life's intriguing little mysteries. She was wearing a hat, something else that was becoming unusual, especially in the morning. Her string bag contained a chicken, butter, eggs, celery, leeks . . .

And something hard, lower down, that kept bumping his thigh with every jolt of the bus: potatoes, no doubt.

Why take the bus to go far from home to buy such ordinary groceries, of a kind to be found in every district of Paris? Perhaps she had once lived on Boulevard Voltaire and, being used to the tradesmen there, had remained faithful to them.

To his right, a young man was smoking a pipe that was too short, too thick and thus badly balanced, which obliged him to clamp his jaws on it. Young men almost always choose a pipe that's too short and thick.

The passengers travelling on the platform were closely packed together. That woman should have gone to sit down inside the bus. Look! Whiting for sale in a fishmonger's on Rue du Temple. It was a long time since he'd eaten whiting. Why was it that, in his mind, whiting, too, was associated with the spring?

Everything was spring-like today, including his mood,

and never mind that the woman with the chicken was staring fixedly ahead, prey to problems that did not trouble ordinary mortals.

'Sorry.'

'Not at all.'

He didn't have the courage to say to her:

'Instead of being a nuisance to everyone, why don't you go and sit down inside, with your shopping?'

He could read the same thought in the blue eyes of a bulky man wedged between himself and the conductor. They understood each other. The conductor, too, gave an imperceptible shrug of his shoulders. A sort of freemasonry between men. It was amusing.

The street stalls, especially those laden with vegetables, spilled out over the pavements. The green and white bus had to weave its way through the crowd of housewives, typists and clerks hurrying to their offices. Life was sweet.

Another jolt. The shopping bag yet again, and whatever that solid thing was, potatoes or some such. Stepping back, he bumped unavoidably into someone behind him.

'Sorry.'

He too murmured an apology, tried to crane round, and glimpsed the face of a young man, a face marked by an emotion that was hard to read.

He could be no more than twenty-five, unshaven and hatless, and his dark hair was tousled. He looked as if he had not slept, and had recently been through some difficult or painful ordeal.

Threading his way towards the step, the same young man jumped from the bus as it was still moving. They had reached the corner of Rue Rambuteau, not far from Les Halles, the central market, whose strong smells pervaded the air. The young man was walking quickly now, turning round as if afraid of something, then he vanished down Rue des Blancs-Manteaux.

And suddenly, for no precise reason, Maigret clapped his hand to his hip pocket where he usually kept his wallet.

He almost jumped off the bus in turn, because the wallet had gone.

His face flushed, but he managed to stay calm. Only the fat man with blue eyes seemed to realize something had happened.

Maigret's own smile was ironic, not so much because he had just been the victim of a pickpocket, but because it was completely impossible for him to give chase.

On account of the spring, precisely, and of the air like champagne that he had started to breathe in the day before.

Another tradition, an obsession dating to his childhood, was new shoes. Every spring, at the first fine days, he would buy slip-on shoes, the lightest available. Which he had done the previous day.

This morning he was wearing them for the first time. And they pinched. Just walking along Boulevard Richard-Lenoir had been agony and he had reached the bus stop on Boulevard Voltaire with relief.

He would have been quite incapable of running after the thief. And the latter had in any case had plenty of time to disappear into the narrow streets of the Marais.

'Sorry, monsieur.'

Again! That woman and her shopping bag! This time, he almost burst out with:

'Why can't you stop banging into other people with your wretched potatoes?'

But he confined himself to a nod and a smile.

In his office too, he encountered that special light of the first fine days, while over the Seine hung a slight mist without the thickness of fog, a mist of millions of bright dancing drops, peculiar to Paris.

'Everything all right, chief? Nothing to report?'

Janvier was wearing a light-coloured suit that Maigret had not seen before. He too was celebrating spring a little early, since it was only 15 March.

'No. Or rather yes. I've just been robbed.'

'Your watch?'

'My wallet.'

'In the street?'

'On the platform of the bus.'

'Was there much money in it?'

'Only about fifty francs. I don't carry more than that as a rule.'

'Your identity papers?'

'Not just my papers, but my badge!'

The famous badge of the Police Judiciaire, a nightmare for any inspector. In theory, they were supposed to carry it at all times, so that they could prove at any moment that they were members of the criminal investigation department.

It was a splendid badge, made of silver, or rather silver-plated bronze, since the thin layer of silver quickly wore off, leaving it a reddish-brown colour.

On one side was an image of Marianne in a Phrygian cap, the initials RF, for République Française, and the word 'Police' framed in red enamel. On the other side, the Paris coat of arms, a number and, engraved in small letters, the holder's name.

Maigret's badge had the number 0004, since number 1 was for the prefect of police, number 2 for the director of the Police Judiciaire, and number 3, for some reason, that of the head of Special Branch.

Everyone was reluctant to carry the badge in a pocket, despite the rules, since the same regulations provided for the suspension of a month's pay if the badge was lost.

'Did you see the thief?'

'Quite clearly. A young man, thin, tired-looking, someone who hadn't slept, judging by his eyes and his complexion.'

'You didn't recognize him?'

In the days when he worked on Street Patrol, Maigret had known by sight all the pickpockets, not only those of Paris, but some who came from Spain or London when there were festivals or major public events.

It was a rather exclusive speciality, with its own hierarchy. Topnotch pickpockets stirred themselves to travel only if the journey was worth it, but then did not hesitate to cross the Atlantic, for a World's Fair, for example, or the Olympic Games.

Maigret had rather lost sight of them now. He searched

his memory. He was not taking the incident too tragically. The light-heartedness of the morning was still influencing his mood and, paradoxically, it was the woman and her shopping bag with whom he felt the most annoyed.

'If only she hadn't kept bumping into me all the time . . . Women shouldn't be allowed on the platform . . . Especially since she didn't have the excuse of needing to smoke . . .'

He was more vexed than really angry.

'You could take a look at the records, perhaps?'

'Yes, that's what I'll do.'

He spent almost an hour examining the photographs, full face and profile, of most of the known pickpockets. There were some he had arrested twenty-five years earlier and who had come through his office ten or fifteen times, almost becoming familiar acquaintances.

'You again?'

'Man's got to live, chief. You're still here too. We go back a bit, don't we?'

Some of them were well dressed; others, of shabbier appearance, were content to work the scrap-metal fairs, the flea market at Saint-Ouen, or the corridors of the Métro. None of them looked anything like the young man on the bus, and Maigret knew in advance that his search would be in vain.

A professional would not have had that tired and anxious look. A practised pickpocket would work only when he could be sure his hands wouldn't tremble. And in any case, they all knew Maigret by sight, his face, his silhouette, if only from the newspapers.

He went back down to his office and, when he found Janvier again, simply shrugged his shoulders.

'You didn't find him?'

'I'm prepared to bet he was an amateur. I even wonder whether he knew he was going to do it a minute beforehand. He must have seen my wallet sticking out of my back pocket. My wife's always telling me not to keep it there. When the bus jolted and those dratted potatoes threw me off balance, he must have suddenly got the idea.'

He changed tone.

'Right, what's new this morning?'

'Lucas is down with flu. And someone bumped off that Senegalese gangster in a café near Porte d'Italie.'

'A stabbing?'

'Naturally. No one can describe the killer. He came in at about one a.m., when the owner was shutting up shop. He went straight over to the Senegalese, who was having one last glass, and struck so quickly that . . .'

One of those routine crimes. Someone would probably grass on him, perhaps in a month, perhaps in two years' time. Maigret headed towards the office of the chief of police for the daily briefing, and took good care not to mention his misadventure.

It was turning out to be a quiet day. Paperwork. Forms to sign. Routine.

He went home for lunch and looked inquiringly at his wife, who had not raised the subject of her driving lesson. It was a bit like going back to school, at her age. She enjoyed it, and was even a little proud of it, but at the same time, she felt embarrassed.

'You managed not to drive up on to the pavement?'

'Why do you have to say that? You'll give me complexes.'

'No, no. You'll make an excellent driver, and I'm waiting impatiently for you to take us for a trip along the Loire.'

'Well, that will have to wait at least a good month, or more.'

'Is that what the instructor said?'

'The examiners are getting more and more exacting, and it's better not to be failed first time. Today, we went on the outer boulevards. Who'd have thought there was so much traffic, and they all drive so fast . . . It's as if . . .'

Ah, they were going to have chicken for lunch, like the woman on the bus no doubt.

'What are you thinking about?'

'My thief.'

'You've arrested a thief?'

'No, I didn't arrest him, but he stole my wallet.'

'With your badge in it?'

That was the first thing she had thought of too. A serious hole in the budget. It was true that he would get a new badge, where the copper wouldn't be showing through.

'And you saw him?'

'As clearly as I'm seeing you.'

'Was he old?'

'Young. An amateur. He looked . . .'

Maigret was thinking about it more and more, without wanting to. Instead of becoming vaguer in his mind's eye, the thief's face was getting clearer. He was remembering details he did not know he had registered, such as that the stranger had thick eyebrows, which met over his eyes.

'Would you know him again?'

He thought about the thief over a dozen times during the afternoon, looking up at the window as if troubled by some problem. In the whole incident, the face, the flight, there was something unnatural, but he couldn't work out what it was. Each time, it seemed that a new detail was going to occur to him, that he would understand, and then he would return to work.

'Goodnight, boys.'

He left at five to six, while there were still half a dozen inspectors in the next office.

'Goodnight, chief.'

He and his wife went to the cinema. He had found in a drawer an old brown wallet, too big for the hip pocket, so he put it inside his jacket.

'Now if you'd been carrying it in *that* pocket . . .'

They walked home, arm in arm as usual, and the air was still quite warm. Even the smell of petrol did not seem so unpleasant tonight. It was part of the arrival of spring, just as the smell of melting tar heralds the arrival of summer.

In the morning, the sun was back again, and he ate his breakfast by the open window.

'Funny thing,' he remarked, 'there are some women who go halfway across Paris by bus, just to buy their groceries.'

'Perhaps that's because of Telex-Consumers.'

He frowned inquiringly at his wife.

'Every night, they tell you on television which neighbourhoods have the best prices for certain things.'

He hadn't thought of that. How simple it was! He had wasted time on a little problem his wife had solved in an instant.

'Thank you.'

'Does that help?'

'It helps me not to think any more about it.'

And, as he picked up his hat, he remarked philosophically:

'You don't always think about what you want to.'

The mail delivery was waiting on his desk and on top of the pile lay a thick brown envelope on which his name, title and the address at Quai des Orfèvres were printed in large capital letters.

He realized what it was before opening it. His wallet was being returned. And a few moments later, he discovered that nothing was missing, not the badge, nor his papers, nor the fifty francs.

There was nothing else. No message. No explanation.

He felt thoroughly vexed at this.

It was a little after eleven when the telephone rang.

'Someone who's insisting on speaking to you personally, sir, but is refusing to give his name. Apparently you'll be expecting this call, and you'll be furious if I don't put it through. What shall I do?'

'Put it through to me, then.'

And striking a match one-handed to relight his pipe:

'Hello. I'm listening.'

There was a rather long silence, and Maigret would have thought he had been cut off if he had not heard breathing at the other end.

'I'm listening,' he repeated.

Another silence, then finally:

'It's me.'

A man's voice, quite deep even, but the tone could have been that of a child hesitating to own up to some piece of mischief.

'My wallet?'

'Yes.'

'You didn't know who I was?'

'Of course not, if I had . . .'

'So why are you telephoning?'

'Because I need to see you.'

'Come to my office, in that case.'

'No, I don't want to go to Quai des Orfèvres.'

'Why not, are you already known here?'

'No, never set foot there.'

'So what are you afraid of, then?'

Since he could sense fear in this anonymous voice.

'It's personal.'

'What's personal?'

'What I want to see you about. I thought of trying this when I read your name on the badge.'

'Why did you steal my wallet?'

'Because I needed money in a hurry.'

'And now?'

'I changed my mind. I'm not so sure. But you'd better come as soon as possible. Before I change my mind again.'

There was something unreal about this conversation and yet Maigret was taking it seriously.

'Where are you?'

'Will you come here?'

'Yes.'

'Alone?'

'Are you insisting on that?'

'Our conversation has to remain private. Will you promise that?'

'It depends.'

'What on?'

'On what you're going to say.'

Another silence, this time seeming more ominous than the one at the start.

'I want you to give me a chance. Remember it was *me* that phoned *you*. You don't know me. You've no way of tracing me. If you don't come, you'll never know who I am. So on your part, that seems to call for . . .'

He couldn't find the right word.

'A promise?' Maigret suggested.

'Wait. I know what. When I've finished talking to you, you'll give me five minutes to get away, if I ask.'

'I can't commit myself without knowing more. I'm an officer of the Police Judiciaire.'

'If you believe me, there won't be a problem. If you don't believe me, or if you have any doubts, you could just manage to look the other way while I make myself scarce, then you can call your men.'

'Where are you?'

'Do you agree?'

'Yes, I'm prepared to meet you.'

'And you accept my conditions?'

'I'll be alone.'

'But you won't make any promises?'

'No.'

It was impossible to do otherwise, and he waited with some anxiety to see how the other man would react. He must have been in a telephone kiosk on the street or in a café, because there was background noise.

'Have you made up your mind?' said Maigret, getting impatient.

'As if I've got any choice! It's what the newspapers say about you that makes me inclined to trust you. Are they true, all those stories?'

'What stories?'

'That you understand certain things that the police and the law courts don't usually understand, and that in some cases, you've even . . .'

'I've even what?'

'Maybe I'm wrong to go on about it. I don't know. Have you sometimes closed your eyes to something?'

Maigret preferred not to answer this.

'Where are you?'

'A long way from the Police Judiciaire. If I was to tell you now, you'd have time to get me arrested by the local inspectors. You could phone them quickly, and you already know what I look like.'

'How do you know I saw you?'

'I looked back. Our eyes met, you know that perfectly well. I was very scared.'

'Because of the wallet?'

'Not just because of that. Listen. Have someone drive you to the bar called Le Métro on the corner of Boulevard de Grenelle and Avenue de La Motte-Picquet. It'll take you about half an hour. I'll call you there. I won't be far off and I'll come and meet you right away.'

Maigret was opening his mouth to say something but the other man had hung up. He felt as intrigued as he was annoyed, since this was the first time a stranger had treated him so casually, not to say cynically.

Still, he couldn't feel too angry. Throughout this quick-fire conversation, he had sensed an anguish, a desire to reach the right solution, a need to be face to face with the inspector who, in the stranger's mind, was his only possible saviour.

Because he had stolen Maigret's wallet, without knowing who he was!

'Janvier! Is there a car downstairs? I need you to drive me over to the Grenelle neighbourhood.'

Janvier was surprised, since no case on hand, just then, had anything to do with that district.

'It's a personal meeting, with the man who stole my wallet.'

'Traced, then?'

'The wallet, yes, it arrived by post this morning.'

'With your badge inside? That's surprising, you might think someone would want to keep it as a souvenir.'

'No, the badge was there, as well as my papers and the money . . .'

'A practical joke, then?'

'No, on the contrary, I think it's very serious. My pick-pocket has phoned me to say he's waiting to see me.'

'Should I come with you?'

'Come as far as Boulevard de Grenelle. After that, you'll have to disappear, because he wants to see me on my own.'

They drove along the Seine as far as the Pont de Bir-Hakeim and Maigret, without speaking, was content simply to watch the river slipping by. There were building works everywhere, demolition sites, barriers, as there had been the first year he had arrived in Paris. It seemed to start all over again each ten to fifteen years, every time Paris felt it was bursting out of its straitjacket.

'Where shall I drop you off?'

'Here.'

They were on the corner of Boulevard de Grenelle and Rue Saint-Charles.

'Shall I wait for you?'

'Wait half an hour. If I'm not back here by then, you can go to the office or for lunch.'

Janvier was intrigued as well, and it was with a curious expression that he watched the inspector's bulky figure walk away.

The sun was shining directly on to the pavement where gusts of warmth and cooler breaths alternated, as if the air had not been able to make up its mind that it was springtime.

A little girl was selling violets in front of a restaurant. Maigret could see in the distance the corner bar with its sign 'Le Métro', which would light up at night. An ordinary-looking café, without any particular character, one of those bars combined with a tobacconist's where you might go in for a packet of cigarettes, to have a drink at the counter, or perhaps to sit at a table if you had arranged to meet someone.

He looked round the interior where no more than twenty café tables were ranged either side of the counter, most of them unoccupied.

The pickpocket of yesterday was not there, of course. The inspector went to sit in the back, near a window, and ordered a draught beer.

In spite of himself, he kept an eye on the door, noticing anyone who approached, pushed it open, and came up to the till, behind which there were shelves full of cigarette packets.

He was starting to wonder whether he had been naive when he recognized a silhouette on the pavement, and then a face. The man did not look at him but went straight up to the counter, leaned on it and ordered:

'A rum.'

He was nervous. His hands were moving all the time. He dared not turn round and showed impatience to be served, as if he urgently needed the alcohol.

Grabbing his glass, he signalled to the waiter not to put the bottle back in its place.

'Same again.'

This time, he did turn towards Maigret. He had known before coming in exactly where the inspector was sitting. He must have been spying on him from outside, or from the window of a nearby house.

He looked apologetic, as if he had had no choice, and had come as soon as he could. With his still trembling hands, he counted out some small change on to the bar.

At last, he moved forwards, took hold of a chair and collapsed into it.

'Have you got any cigarettes?'

'No, I only smoke a—'

'A pipe, yes I know. I don't have any cigarettes left, and I've run out of money.'

'Waiter! A packet of – what kind do you like?'

'Gauloises.'

'A packet of Gauloises and a glass of rum.'

'No, no more rum, it'll make me feel sick.'

'A beer, then?'

'I don't know. I haven't eaten anything this morning . . .'

'A sandwich?'

There were several plates of sandwiches on the counter.

'Not just now. I feel like I'm choking. You can't understand . . .'

He was quite well dressed: grey flannel trousers and a checked sports jacket.

Like many young men, he was wearing a polo-neck sweater, rather than a shirt and tie.

'I don't know if you're quite what I was expecting from your reputation.'

He was not looking Maigret in the face, but darting quick glances at him before staring down at the floor once more. It was tiring to follow the constant movement of his long, thin fingers.

'You weren't surprised to get the wallet back?'

'After thirty years in the police, not much surprises me.'

'With the money still inside it?'

'You desperately needed cash, didn't you?'

'Yes.'

'How much did you have in your pocket, then?'

'About ten francs.'

'Where did you sleep last night?'

'I didn't sleep anywhere. I didn't eat either. I spent the ten francs on drink. You just saw me use up the last few coins. It wasn't enough to get drunk on.'

'But you live in Paris,' Maigret remarked.

'How do you know that?'

'And indeed, in this district.'

They had no immediate neighbours and were speaking in low voices. The door of the café could be heard opening and shutting, almost always for customers buying tobacco or matches.

'But you didn't go home.'

The young man was silent for a moment, as he had been on the telephone. He looked pale and exhausted. Evidently, he was making a desperate effort to respond and, full of suspicion, he was trying to foresee any traps that might be laid for him.

'Just as I thought,' he muttered finally.

'What did you think?'

'That you'd guess, you'd be more or less right, and once I was hooked . . .'

'Go on.'

He suddenly became angry and raised his voice, forgetting he was in a public place.

'And once I was hooked, I'd be done for, wouldn't I!'

He looked towards the door, which happened to be opening just then, and for a moment Maigret thought he was going to run away again. He must have been tempted. There had been a quick flash in his dark brown eyes. Then he reached out for the glass of beer, and drank it off in a single gulp, all the while observing the inspector over the top of the glass, as if judging him.

'Better now?'

'I don't know yet.'

'Let's get back to the wallet.'

'Why?'

'Because that was what made you telephone me.'

'There wasn't enough in it anyway.'

'Enough money? What for?'

'To get away . . . To go somewhere else, anywhere, Belgium, Spain . . .'

And then, looking suspicious again:

'You did come on your own, didn't you?'

'I don't drive. One of my inspectors brought me over here and he's waiting for me at the corner of Rue Saint-Charles.'

The man raised his head suddenly.

'You've identified me?'

'No, your photo isn't on file.'

'But you did look?'

'Of course.'

'Why?'

'Because of the wallet, but especially because of my badge.'

'Why did you stop at the corner of Rue Saint-Charles?'

'Because it's near here, and it was on our way.'

'You haven't had a report?'

'What about?'

'About an incident in Rue Saint-Charles?'

Maigret found it hard to follow the expressions succeeding one another on the young man's face. Rarely had he come across anyone so anxious, so anguished, clinging obstinately on to heaven only knew what hope.

He was afraid, that was clear. But of what?

'The police station here didn't contact you?'

'No.'

'Do you swear it?'

'The only time I swear is in the witness box.'

The young man seemed to want to drill into him with his eyes.

'Why do you think I asked you to come?'

'Because you need me.'

'And why do I need you?'

'Because you're in some kind of trouble and you don't know how to get out of it.'

'That's not true.'

The voice was firm. The unknown young man lifted up his head, as if relieved.

'It's not me that's in trouble, and I'll swear that, in court or anywhere else. I'm innocent, do you hear me?'

'Not so loud.'

He looked round. A young woman was applying lipstick while peering in a mirror, then turning towards the street in the hope of seeing the man she was waiting for.

24

Two middle-aged men, leaning their heads together over a table, were talking in low voices and, from the few words he guessed at rather than heard, Maigret gathered the subject was horse-racing.

'Well, tell me who you are, and what it is you say you're innocent of.'

'Not here. Not now.'

'Where, then?'

'Back at my place. Can I have another beer? I'll be able to pay you back, soon, unless . . .'

'Unless?'

'Unless, her bag . . . Anyway . . . a beer?'

'Waiter! Two beers. And the bill.'

The young man wiped his forehead with a handkerchief that was still quite clean.

'You're twenty-four?' the inspector asked him.

'Twenty-five.'

'So how long have you lived in Paris?'

'Five years.'

'Married?'

He was avoiding asking questions that were too personal and intimate.

'I was. Why do you ask?'

'You don't wear a wedding ring.'

'Because when I got married, I couldn't afford one.'

He lit another cigarette. He had smoked the first with long, deep pulls, and only now was he appreciating the taste of tobacco.

'So all the precautions I took didn't work.'

'What precautions?'

'About you. You've got your hands on me, whatever I do. Even if I tried to run off, now you've seen me close up, and you know I live nearby.'

He was smiling ironically, the bitter irony addressed to himself.

'I always overdo things. Is your inspector in the car still on the corner of Rue Saint-Charles?'

Maigret looked at the electric clock on the wall. Three minutes to midday.

'Either he's just left or he will be leaving any minute, because I asked him to wait half an hour and, if I wasn't back, to go for lunch.'

'It doesn't matter, though, does it?'

Maigret did not reply and when his companion rose to go, he followed. They went together towards Rue Saint-Charles, at the corner of which there was a fairly new modern building. They crossed over, turned down the street and walked only about thirty metres further.

The man had stopped in the middle of the pavement, opposite a wide carriage door giving on to the courtyard of the large apartment block that went through to Boulevard de Grenelle; cycles and babies' prams were stored under an archway.

'You live here?'

'Listen, inspector . . .'

He was paler and more nervous than ever.

'Have you ever trusted somebody, even when all the evidence was against him?'

'It has happened.'

'What do you think of me?'

'That you're rather complicated, and that I don't have enough elements to make a judgement.'

'Because you will make a judgement?'

'That wasn't what I meant. Let's say, to form an opinion about you.'

'Do I look like a criminal?'

'Certainly not.'

'Or a man capable of . . . no, come inside. Best get it over with.'

He drew Maigret inside the courtyard and towards the left-hand side of the building, where at ground level there was a series of doors.

'They call these "bachelor flats",' the young man muttered.

He took a key from his pocket.

'You're going to make me go in first. Well, I'll do it, whatever it costs. But if I pass out . . .'

He pushed open a varnished wooden door. It gave on to a tiny entrance hall. Through an open door on the right could be seen a bathroom with a half-size bath. The room was in some disorder: towels were scattered on the tiled floor.

'Will *you* open it?'

The young man gestured to Maigret to open the firmly shut door ahead of them, and Maigret did as he was asked.

His companion did not run away. And yet the smell was terrible, despite the open window.

Alongside a sofa-bed, a young woman was lying on the multicoloured Moroccan carpet: over her body buzzed a cloud of bluebottle flies . . .

2.

'Do you have a telephone?'

It was a ridiculous question, and Maigret had uttered it without thinking, since he could now see the telephone on the floor in the middle of the room, about a metre away from the body.

'Oh, please, I beg you . . .' the young man was murmuring, as he leaned against the door-jamb.

He was clearly at the end of his tether. Maigret too was not unwilling to leave the room, where the smell of death was unbearable.

He propelled the young man outside, closed the door behind him, and took a moment to regain consciousness of the real world.

Children were coming home from school, swinging their satchels and heading towards other apartments. Most of the windows in the large block were open. The sound of several radios could be heard at once, voices, music, and women calling to their sons or husbands. On the first floor, a canary was hopping about in its cage and elsewhere clothes were drying on a line.

'Are you going to be sick?'

The other man shook his head, but didn't yet dare open his mouth. He was pressing both hands to his chest, pale as death, and was about to collapse, to judge by the almost convulsive movements of his fingers and the uncontrolled trembling of his lips.

'Take your time. Don't try to speak. Shall we get a drink of something in the café?'

Another shake of the head.

'She's your wife, isn't she?'

His eyes said yes. He opened his mouth to take in a breath of air, managing to do so only after a moment, as if his nerves were completely jangled.

'And you were there when it happened?'

'No.'

He had all the same managed to get that syllable out.

'When did you last see her?'

'Day before yesterday . . . Wednesday . . .'

'Morning? Evening?'

'Late that night.'

They were pacing automatically up and down in the large sunlit courtyard, while in all the lodgings around them, people were leading their everyday lives. Most of them were already eating their midday meal, or were about to. Snatches of conversation reached them:

'Have you washed your hands?'

'Mind out, it's hot.'

Through the springtime air wafted cooking smells, leeks in particular.

'And do you know how she died?'

The young man nodded, without speaking, since he was once more unable to breathe.

'When I came back . . .'

'Wait a minute. You left the flat late on Wednesday

night . . . Keep walking . . . Standing still won't help . . .
About what time?'

'Eleven.'

'And your wife was alive then? And in her dressing
gown?'

'No, she hadn't undressed yet.'

'You work nights?'

'No, I was going out to look for some money. We were
desperate.'

They were both walking round the yard, their eyes
roving unseeingly over the open windows around them,
from some of which people peered out, no doubt wondering what they were doing there.

'Where did you think you would get any money?'

'From friends. Here and there.'

'But you didn't find any?'

'No.'

'Did some of your friends see you?'

'In the Vieux-Pressoir, yes. I still had about thirty francs
in my pocket. I went round to different places where there
was a chance of finding someone.'

'On foot?'

'No, in my car. I left it on the corner of Rue François-Ier
and Rue Marbeuf when I ran out of petrol.'

'So what did you do then?'

'I went on foot.'

The young man in front of Maigret was exhausted, a
hyper-sensitive character, ready to twitch at any touch.

'When did you last eat anything?'

'I had two hard-boiled eggs in a café yesterday.'

'Well, come along, then.'

'I'm not hungry. If you're trying to take me to lunch, let me tell you right away . . .'

Maigret took no notice, moving them both towards Boulevard de Grenelle and entering a little restaurant where there were some free tables.

'Two steak and chips,' he ordered.

He wasn't hungry either, but his companion needed to eat.

'What's your name?'

'Ricain, François Ricain. Some people call me Francis. It's my wife who . . .'

'Look here, Ricain, I'm going to have to make a few phone calls.'

'To your colleagues?'

'In the first place, I'll have to inform the local police chief, then the prosecutor's office. Will you promise not to move from here?'

'Where would I go?' Ricain replied bitterly. 'Whatever happens, you're going to arrest me and send me to prison. I won't be able to bear it, I'd rather . . .'

He didn't finish the sentence, but the end could be guessed.

'Waiter! A half-bottle of red.'

Maigret went to the counter to get tokens for the telephone. As he expected, the local police chief had gone for lunch.

'Should I pass the message on right away?'

'When will he be back?'

'About two o'clock.'

'Tell him I'll be expecting him at quarter past two in Rue Saint-Charles, outside the street door to a building on the corner of Boulevard de Grenelle.'

At the prosecutor's office, he only managed to reach a junior official.

'A crime appears to have been committed in Rue Saint-Charles . . . Take down the address . . . When one of the deputies comes back, tell him I'll be in front of the street door at quarter past two.'

Finally he rang the Police Judiciaire, and Lapointe picked up the call.

'Can you be here in an hour? Rue Saint-Charles . . . Contact Police Records and have them get to the same address by about two . . . Tell them to bring something to disinfect the room, because the smell of decomposition is so strong it's impossible to go in. And tell the police pathologist . . . I don't know who will be on duty today . . . See you soon.'

He went back to sit down opposite Ricain, who had not budged, and who was gazing round as if he couldn't believe in the reality of the everyday sight.

It was a modest restaurant. Most of the customers were men who worked locally and were eating alone, reading their newspapers. The steaks arrived and the chips were crisp.

'What's going to happen now?' asked the young man, who had automatically picked up his fork. 'You've told everybody? There's going to be a big fuss?'

'Not until two o'clock. Until then we can have a few words between ourselves.'

'I don't know anything . . .'

'People always think they don't know anything.'

It was best not to push him too far. After a few minutes, as Maigret was about to put a piece of meat in his mouth, François Ricain began, without seeming to think about it, to cut up his steak.

He'd said he wouldn't be able to eat. Not only did he eat, but he also drank some wine and, a few minutes later, the inspector had to order another half-bottle.

'But you won't understand . . .'

'Of all the sentences people say, that's the one I've heard most often in the course of my career. And nine times out of ten, I *have* understood . . .'

'I know, you're going to make me blurt out something incriminating . . .'

'*Is* there something incriminating?'

'Don't make a joke of it. You saw, the same as I did.'

'Except that you had seen that sight already once. Is that right?'

'Of course.'

'When?'

'Yesterday, at about four a.m.'

'Wait, let me get this straight. The day before yesterday, that is Wednesday, you went out at about eleven at night, leaving your wife inside the apartment . . .?'

'Sophie wanted to come with me, she was insisting. I made her stay home, because I don't like begging for money in her presence. It would be as if I was using her to get it.'

'Very well. You went off in your car. What kind of car is it?'

'A Triumph Convertible.'

'If you needed money as badly as all that, why not sell it?'

'Because I wouldn't have got a hundred francs for it. It's a beat-up old car I bought second-hand, with God knows how many previous owners. It could hardly hold the road.'

'So you looked for some friends who might be in a position to lend you some money, but you didn't find them?'

'The ones I did find were almost as broke as me.'

'And you came home on foot at four a.m. Did you knock at the door?'

'No, I opened it with my key.'

'Had you been drinking?'

'I'd had a few, yes. In the evening, the kind of people I know are going to be in bars or nightclubs.'

'Were you drunk?'

'No, I wasn't that far gone.'

'Discouraged?'

'I was at my wits' end.'

'Did your wife have any money?'

'No more than me. She might have had about twenty or thirty francs in her handbag.'

'Go on . . . Waiter! More chips, please.'

'I found her lying on the floor. When I went closer, I saw that half her face was . . . blown away. I think I could see grey matter . . .'

He pushed his plate away and drank thirstily from his fourth glass of wine.

'I'm sorry . . . I'd rather not talk about it.'

'Was there a gun in the flat?'

Ricain sat still, staring at Maigret as if the crucial moment had arrived.

'A revolver, perhaps? Or an automatic?'

'Yes.'

'An automatic?'

'It was mine. A Browning 6.35, manufactured in Herstal.'

'How did you come to have this weapon in your possession?'

'I was waiting for you to ask me that. And you probably won't believe this . . .'

'You didn't buy it from a gunsmith?'

'No, I had no reason to go out and buy a pistol. It happened one night, out with friends in a little restaurant at La Villette. We'd drunk a lot. We were pretending to be gangsters.'

He had blushed.

'Especially me . . . The others will tell you . . . It's an obsession . . . When I've drunk a lot, I think I'm a great guy . . . Well, some people we didn't know came over and joined us. You know how it is on a night out. It was in winter two years ago. I was wearing this big sheepskin jacket. Sophie was with me. She'd had a few drinks too, but she never quite loses control.

'Next day, about twelve, when I went to put my jacket on, I found the automatic in the pocket. My wife said I had bought it the night before, not listening to her protests. Apparently I'd been claiming I was going to shoot someone who was mad at me. I kept saying:

' "It's him or me, old man . . ." '

Maigret, having lit his pipe, looked at his companion, his expression giving nothing away of his reaction.

'Can you understand that?'

'Carry on . . . It's now Thursday, four in the morning. I presume no one could have seen you go into your apartment?'

'No, of course not.'

'Nor seen you come out.'

'No, no one.'

'What did you do with the gun?'

'How do you know I got rid of it?'

The inspector shrugged his shoulders.

'I don't know why I did it. I realized I would be accused . . .'

'Why?'

Ricain looked at the inspector in amazement.

'Well, it's natural, isn't it? I was the only person who had a key. Someone had used a gun that belonged to me, that I kept in a drawer in the chest. Sophie and I had quarrelled in the past. She wanted me to get a steady job.'

'What *do* you do?'

'If you can call it a job, I'm a journalist, but I'm not attached to any particular paper. In other words, I place my copy wherever I can – mostly film reviews. I'm also an assistant director and occasionally I work on screenplays.'

'So you threw the Browning in the Seine?'

'Yes, a bit beyond the Pont de Bir-Hakeim. Then I just walked.'

'Did you go on looking for your friends?'

'I didn't dare any more. Someone might have heard the shot and called the police. I don't know. At a time like that, you aren't always thinking straight.

'I was certain to be a wanted man. I'd be accused, and everything would tell against me, even the fact that I'd been wandering about part of the night. I'd been drinking. I kept looking for any bar that was still open. When I found one, in Rue Vaugirard, I drank three glasses of rum on the trot . . .

'If I'd been questioned, I was in no state to give answers. I would have muddled things up, for sure. They'd shut me in a cell. But I suffer from claustrophobia, I can't even take the Métro. And the idea of prison, with big bolts on the door . . .'

'Was it the claustrophobia that gave you the idea of escaping somewhere abroad?'

'See, you don't believe me!'

'Perhaps I do.'

'You'd have to have been in a situation like I was to know what goes through your head. You don't think logically . . . I couldn't tell you where I went altogether. I needed to walk. To get away from Grenelle, because I thought they'd be looking for me there. I remember seeing Gare Montparnasse. I had a white wine on Boulevard Saint-Michel . . . or was it at Gare Montparnasse?

'It wasn't exactly that I wanted to escape. I just needed some time, so as not to be questioned by the police, the state I was in. In Belgium or somewhere, I could have waited a bit. Read the newspapers about the investigation.

I'd have learned details I didn't know, so it would have made it easier to defend myself.'

Maigret could not help smiling at such a mixture of cunning and naivety.

'So what were you doing on Place de la République?'

'I don't know. I just ended up there, could have been anywhere. I had one ten-franc note in my pocket. I let three buses go past.'

'Because they were the kind that are closed in?'

'I don't know. I swear, inspector, I don't know . . . I needed money if I was going to get a train. I got up on to the platform of the bus. There were a lot of people, we were squashed together. I could only see you from behind.

'At one point, you stepped backwards and almost lost your balance. I saw the wallet sticking out of your pocket. I just grabbed it, without thinking, and when I looked up, I saw a woman, staring at me.

'I've no idea why she didn't raise the alarm at once. I jumped off the bus while it was moving. Luckily it was a crowded area, and the streets around there are narrow and twisting. I ran, then I walked.'

'Waiter, can you get us two pastries?'

It was half past one. In forty-five minutes, the wheels of justice would begin to turn as usual, and the small flat in Rue Saint-Charles would be invaded by officials, while uniformed police would be keeping curious onlookers away.

'What are you going to do with me now?'

Maigret didn't answer at once, for the good reason that he had not made up his mind.

'Are you going to arrest me? I know you don't have any choice, but I swear to you again that . . .'

'Eat up. Do you want a coffee?'

'Why are you doing this?'

'What's so odd about it?'

'You're making me eat and drink. You haven't bullied me, on the contrary, you've been listening to me patiently. Is this the kind of questioning they say makes canaries sing?'

Maigret smiled.

'Not quite, no. I'm just trying to get things clear in my head . . .'

'And to get me to talk . . .'

'I didn't put any pressure on you.'

'Well anyway, for the moment, I feel a bit better.'

He had eaten the pastry as if without noticing and now lit a cigarette. There was more colour in his cheeks.

'But look, I can't face going back there, seeing, smelling . . .'

'Well, I have to.'

'It's your job. And she wasn't your wife.'

He veered from incoherent muttering to perfectly good common sense, from blind panic to lucid reasoning.

'You're a strange young man.'

'Because I'm sincere?'

'Look, *I* don't want to have you under my feet either when the authorities get here, and still less do I want you to be harassed by journalists. When my inspectors get to Rue Saint-Charles – they're probably waiting for us already – I'll have you driven to Quai des Orfèvres.'

'To a cell?'

'No, to my office, where you will oblige me by waiting quietly.'

'And then? What'll happen next?'

'That depends.'

'What do you hope to discover?'

'I've no idea. I know even less about this than you, because I didn't look closely at her body and I haven't seen the gun.'

This entire conversation was accompanied by the sounds of glasses and forks, the murmur of voices, the coming and going of the waiter, and the tinny bell on the cash register.

The sun was lighting the other side of the street, where the shadows of passers-by were short and squat. Cars, taxis, buses drove past constantly, doors slammed.

As they left the restaurant, both men hesitated. In their corner of the bistro, they had for a long while been cut off from other people, from daily life, all the familiar sounds, voices and images.

'Do you believe me?'

Ricain was asking the same question again, not daring to look at Maigret.

'This isn't the moment to go into believing or not believing. Look! My men have arrived.'

He could see in Rue Saint-Charles one of the black cars belonging to the Police Judiciaire, as well as the van of the Police Records department, and he recognized Lapointe in the little group that stood talking on the pavement. The sturdy Torrence was there as well, and it was to him that Maigret passed his companion.

'Take him to headquarters. Install him in my office, and stay with him. Don't be surprised if he drops off to sleep – he hasn't had a wink for two nights.'

Shortly after two o'clock, a van drove up from the Paris city sanitation service, since Moers and his men did not have the necessary equipment.

By then, in the courtyard, several groups of men were waiting outside the front doors of the ground-floor apartments, while bystanders, kept at some distance by uniformed police, were observing the scene with curiosity.

In one group, the deputy prosecutor Dréville and the examining magistrate Camus were chatting to Piget, the chief of police in the fifteenth arrondissement. All of them had come straight from their lunch, which had no doubt been quite copious, and since the disinfection process was taking some time, every now and again they checked their watches.

The duty pathologist was Doctor Delaplanque, fairly new to the profession, but Maigret liked him and was now asking him a few questions. Delaplanque had not hesitated, despite the smell and the flies, to make an initial examination of the body in the bedroom.

'I'll be able to tell you more presently. You mentioned a 6.35 pistol, which is a bit surprising, since I'd be inclined to bet the wound came from something bigger.'

'What distance?'

'At first sight, there isn't a ring of gunpowder round the site of entry. Death was instantaneous or almost so, because the woman lost very little blood. Who is she, by the way?'

'The wife of a young journalist.'

For all these people, as for Moers and the specialists of the forensic team, this was all in a day's work, and carried out without any visible emotion. Indeed, one of the men from the city sanitation service had exclaimed on entering the flat:

'Phew, this dame stinks, eh!'

Some women onlookers had babies in their arms, others, well placed to see everything without stirring, stayed leaning on their window-sills, and comments were passed from one lodging to another.

'Are you sure he isn't the fat one?'

'No, the fat one, I don't know who that is.'

They were referring to Inspector Lourtie. But it was Maigret that the two women were searching for.

'Look, he's the one smoking a pipe.'

'There are two of them smoking pipes.'

'Not the young one, of course. The other one. Look, he's going over to those people from the Palais de Justice.'

Deputy prosecutor Déville was asking Maigret:

'Any idea what this is all about?'

'The dead woman is Sophie Ricain, née Le Gal, aged twenty-two, originally from Concarneau, where her father is a watchmaker.'

'Has he been informed?'

'Not yet. I'll see to it presently.'

'Married?'

'Yes, for three years, to François Ricain, a young journalist. He does a bit of film work, and is trying to make a career in Paris.'

'Where is he now?'

'In my office.'

'Is he a suspect?'

'Not at the moment. He's in no state to answer questions from a magistrate, and he'd just get in the way here.'

'Where was he when the crime was committed?'

'We don't know the time of the crime yet.'

'Doctor, can you give us a rough idea?'

'No, not yet. Perhaps after the autopsy, if I can find out when the victim ate her last meal and what it consisted of.'

'The neighbours?'

'Plenty of them are watching us, as you can see. I haven't questioned them yet, but I doubt they'll have much of interest to tell us. What you need to know is that it's possible to enter these ground-floor flats without going past the concierge's lodge, because that's at the other entrance, on Boulevard de Grenelle.'

It was a tedious time. They remained waiting. People exchanged meaningless remarks and Lapointe followed his chief about, silently, with the gaze and attitude of a faithful dog.

The sanitation team were bringing out of the apartment a large flexible tube, painted grey, which they had taken in there a quarter of an hour earlier. Their leader, in white overalls, beckoned the police over.

'Don't stay too long in the room,' he warned Maigret, 'there's still a lot of formalin in the air.'

Doctor Delaplanque knelt down by the body and examined it with rather more care than he had the first time.

'As far as I'm concerned, you can take her away.'

'What about you, Maigret?'

Maigret had seen all there was to see: a huddled body in a flowered silk dressing gown. A red mule was still hanging on to one foot. It was impossible from her position in the room to say what the woman had been doing, or even where exactly she had been, when the bullet hit her.

As far as he could judge, her face had been unremarkable, but quite pretty. Her toenails were varnished red, but had not been recently cared for, since the varnish was cracked and the nails were not entirely clean.

Standing alongside his chief, the court clerk was taking notes, as was the secretary of the local police inspector.

'You can bring in the stretcher.'

They crunched over dead flies. One after another, the people who crowded into the room took out handkerchiefs to pat their eyes, because of the formalin.

The body was removed and a respectful silence reigned for a few moments in the courtyard. The men from the prosecutor's office were the first to leave, then Delaplanque, while Moers and his specialists were waiting to start their work.

'We look everywhere, do we, chief?'

'Best to do that. You never know.'

Perhaps this case was a mystery, or perhaps, on the contrary, it would turn out to be entirely straightforward. That's how it is at the start of every investigation, or almost.

Maigret, his eyelids smarting, pulled open the drawer of a chest which contained a clutter of various objects: an old pair of opera glasses, some buttons, a broken pen and some pencils, stills from a film set, sunglasses, bills . . .

He would return when the smell had had time to dissipate, but as of now he was well able to register the strange décor of the little apartment. The floor had been varnished black, the walls and ceiling painted bright scarlet. The furniture by contrast was chalky white, which made the whole interior rather unreal. It was almost like a stage set. Nothing seemed solid.

'What do you think of this, Lapointe? Would you like to live in a room like this?'

'It'd give me nightmares.'

They went out. Some stragglers were still lingering in the courtyard and the police had let them come a little nearer.

'I told you it was that one. I wonder if he'll be back. Apparently he does all the inquiries himself so perhaps he'll come over and question us.'

The speaker, a faded blonde with a baby in her arms, was looking at Maigret with a smile inspired no doubt by a film star.

'I'll leave Lourtie with you. Here's the key to the flat. When Moers' men have finished, lock up and start questioning the neighbours. The crime wasn't committed last night, if crime it was, but during the night from Wednesday to Thursday.

'Try to find out if the neighbours heard any coming and going. Divide the tenants up between you and Lourtie. Then ask the local shopkeepers. There are a lot of bills in the drawer. You'll find the addresses there of the tradesmen they used.

'I almost forgot. Can you check if the phone's working? It seemed to me at midday that it was off the hook.'

The telephone was working.

'Don't come back to headquarters, either of you, without calling me first. Good luck.'

Maigret set off towards Boulevard de Grenelle and went down the steps into the Métro. Half an hour later, he emerged into fresh air and sunshine. He was soon in his office, where François Ricain was meekly waiting while Torrence read a newspaper.

'Aren't you thirsty?' he asked Ricain, as he took off his hat and went to open the window a little wider. 'Nothing to report, Torrence?'

'A newspaperman just phoned.'

'I was surprised they didn't turn up over there. Their information network in the fifteenth must be inefficient. Lapointe will have them on his back by now.'

He turned towards Ricain, looked at his hands, and told the inspector:

'Take him up to the lab for the paraffin test, just to be on the safe side. It won't prove anything, since the crime was committed two days ago, but it'll avoid any awkward questions.'

They would know in a quarter of an hour whether there were traces of gunpowder on Ricain's fingers. Their absence would not indicate absolutely that he had not fired the gun, but it would be a point in his favour.

'Hello . . . Is that you, my dear? . . . I'm very sorry . . . Of course . . . If I hadn't been caught up in a case, I'd have been back for lunch . . . Yes, yes, I ate some steak and chips, with a rather excitable young man. I did tell myself when I went into the restaurant that I'd phone you, but the conversation was non-stop and I confess, it went right out of my head. You're not cross with me, are you? . . . No, I don't know . . . We'll have to see.'

Tonight, he might or might not be home for dinner, he could not yet predict anything. Especially with a man like François Ricain, who changed his mood every few seconds.

Maigret would have found it difficult to formulate an opinion of him. Intelligent, yes, certainly, and highly so, as far as one could tell from what lay beneath some of his utterances. Yet alongside that, there was a naive, rather childish side to him.

How could one judge him at the moment? His condition was morally and physically lamentable; he was a bundle of nerves, torn between warring feelings.

If he had not killed his wife, and if he really had planned to take refuge in Belgium or elsewhere, it pointed to a state of total disorientation, which could not be explained alone by the claustrophobia he had mentioned.

Presumably he was the one responsible for the strange way the apartment was decorated, its black floor, red walls and ceiling, and those pale, ghost-like pieces of furniture that stood out as if floating in space.

It gave the impression that the ground you were walking on was not solid, that the walls were going to move in or out, as in a film studio, that the chest of drawers, the sofa-bed, the table and chairs were all artificial, made of papier-mâché.

And wasn't he a somewhat artificial being himself? Maigret could just imagine the face of the deputy prosecutor or of Camus, the examining magistrate, if they had read at a stretch all the sentences the young man had uttered, first in the café at La Motte-Picquet, and then in the little local restaurant afterwards.

Maigret would have liked to have Doctor Pardon's opinion of him.

Ricain came back into the office, followed by Torrence.

'And?'

'Negative.'

'I've never fired a shot in my life, except at a fairground. I wouldn't even know where to find the safety catch.'

'Sit down.'

'Have you spoken to the examining magistrate?'

'Yes, I saw the examining magistrate and the deputy prosecutor.'

'What did they say? Am I going to be arrested?'

'It must be about the tenth time you've said that word. So far, I would have only one reason to arrest you: the theft of my wallet, and I haven't brought charges.'

'I sent it back to you!'

'Quite true. We're going to try and get straight some things you've told me and others that I don't know yet. You can go, Torrence. Tell Janvier to come in.'

Shortly afterwards, Janvier was sitting at one end of the desk, taking a pencil from his pocket.

'Your name is François Ricain, and you're twenty-five years old. Where were you born?'

'Paris, Rue Caulaincourt.'

A respectable street, almost provincial in character, behind the Sacré-Coeur.

'Are your parents still alive?'

'My father is. He works for the railways, he's an engine driver.'

'How long have you been married?'

'Just over three and a half years. It would have been four in June. The 17th.'

'So you were twenty-one and your wife was . . .?'

'Eighteen.'

'Was your father already widowed then?'

'My mother died when I was fifteen.'

'And you went on living with your father?'

'For a year or two. When I was seventeen I left home.'

'Why?'

'Because we didn't get on.'

'For any particular reason?'

'No . . . I was bored. He wanted me to get a job with the railways too, but I refused. He thought I was wasting my time reading and studying . . .'

'Did you get your baccalauréat?'

'No, I left school two years before that.'

'To do what? Where did you live, and on what sort of income?'

'You're rushing me,' Ricain complained.

'I'm not rushing you, I'm asking you some elementary questions.'

'Different things at different times. I sold newspapers in the street. Then I was an errand boy for a printer in Rue Montmartre. For a while I shared a room with a friend.'

'Name and address?'

'Bernard Fléchier, he had a bedsit in Rue Coquillière. I've lost touch with him now.'

'What was his job?'

'He drove a delivery scooter.'

'And then?'

'I worked for six months in a stationer's shop. I was writing stories and took them to newspapers. One of them was accepted and it earned me a hundred francs. The man I met was surprised I was so young . . .'

'Did he publish any more of your stories?'

'No, the ones after that were turned down.'

'What were you doing when you met your wife, I mean the girl you were going to marry, Sophie Le Gal – that was her name, wasn't it?'

'I was third assistant on a film that got banned by the censor. It was a war film, made by a group of young people.'

'And Sophie was working?'

'Not regularly. She was an extra. She got the occasional modelling job.'

'Did she live alone?'

'She had a hotel room in Saint-Germain-des-Prés.'

'Was it love at first sight?'

'No. We ended up sleeping together because after a party we found ourselves in the street at three a.m. She let me go back with her. We stayed together for some months, then, one fine day, we decided to get married.'

'Did her parents approve?'

'They didn't have much to say about it. She went to Concarneau and came back with a letter from her father allowing us to marry.'

'What about you?'

'I went to see my father too.'

'What did he say?'

'He just shrugged his shoulders.'

'He didn't come to the wedding?'

'No, we just invited some friends, three or four. And in the evening we had a meal all together in Les Halles.'

'Before she met you, did Sophie have anyone else?'

'I wasn't the first, if that's what you're getting at.'

'She didn't live for any length of time before you with a man who might have been sufficiently keen to try and see her again?'

He seemed to search his memory.

'No. We met some of her past boyfriends, but there hadn't been any important love affair. You know, in four years, you move around in different groups. We'd be friendly with some people for six months, and then they'd drop out of our lives. Other people would take their place, and we'd meet up now and again. You ask questions as if it was all quite simple. You're getting my answers written down. If I make a mistake, or leave something out you'll jump to God only knows what conclusions. It's not fair . . .'

'Would you prefer me to question you with a lawyer present?'

'Do I have the right?'

'If you consider that you're a suspect.'

'What about you, how do you consider me?'

'As a man whose wife has died a violent death. As a young fellow who panicked, stole my wallet, then sent it back to me intact. As an intelligent but not very stable person.'

'If you'd spent the last two nights like I did . . .'

'We'll get to that presently. So you did various short-term jobs?'

'It was just to earn a living while I waited . . .'

'Waited for what?'

'To start my career.'

'What kind of career?'

He frowned as he looked at Maigret, as if to assure himself that there was no mockery in the inspector's voice.

'I'm still hesitating. Perhaps I'll do both . . . I certainly want to write, but I'm not sure if it will take the form of screenplays, or whether I'll try novels . . . Directing would tempt me, but only if I could have complete control over the film . . .'

'You have contacts in the film industry?'

'Through the Vieux-Pressoir, yes. You meet beginners like me there. But an important producer like Monsieur Carus isn't too grand to have dinner with us.'

'Who is this Monsieur Carus?'

'A film producer, like I said. He lives in the Hotel Raphaël, and his offices are at 18A, Rue de Bassano, just off the Champs-Élysées.'

'And he puts up the money for films?'

'He's done three or four. Co-productions with the Germans and Italians. He travels around a lot.'

'And how old is this gentleman?'

'Round about forty.'

'Is he married?'

'He lives with a young woman called Nora, an ex-model.'

'Did he know your wife?'

'Of course. This is a scene where we all know each other.'

'Does Monsieur Carus have plenty of money?'

'He finds enough for his films.'

'But he doesn't have personal wealth?'

'Like I said, he lives in the Raphaël, he has a suite of rooms there. It must be expensive. And in the evenings, you'll find him in the most chic nightclubs.'

'It wasn't by any chance him that you were looking for on the night from Wednesday to Thursday?'

Ricain blushed.

'Yes. Well, him or somebody else. Preferably him, because he usually has bundles of notes in his pocket.'

'Do you owe him money?'

'Yes.'

'A lot?'

'Getting on for two thousand . . .'

'And he hasn't asked you to pay it back?'

'No.'

A slight change, difficult to identify with precision, had come over the young man, and Maigret observed him more closely.

But he would have to proceed carefully, since his interviewee was always ready to go back into his shell.

3.

When Maigret stood up, Ricain gave a start and looked at him anxiously, since he always seemed to expect some blow of fate, or some betrayal. The inspector went to stand for a moment at the open window, as if to plunge back into the real world, watching the passers-by, the traffic on the Pont Saint-Michel, and a tug-boat with a large white trefoil on its funnel.

'I'll be right back.'

From the inspectors' office, he called the Forensic Institute.

'Maigret here. Could you see whether Doctor Delaplanque has finished his post-mortem?'

He waited some time before he heard the pathologist's voice on the line.

'Ah, good timing, inspector. I was just going to call you. Have you discovered what time the young woman had her last meal, and what it consisted of?'

'I'll be able to tell you that in a minute. What about the wound?'

'As far as I can judge, the shot was fired from a distance I'd reckon as a metre to a metre and a half.'

'From the front?'

'From the side. The victim was standing. She must have staggered back a step or two before falling on to the carpet. The lab that checked the bloodstains can confirm that. Something else. This woman had begun a pregnancy which was terminated in the third or fourth month, rather clumsily. She was a heavy smoker, but her health generally was quite good.'

'Can you hold on for a moment?'

He went back into his office.

'Did you eat dinner with your wife on Wednesday night?'

'At about half past eight at the Vieux-Pressoir.'

'Can you remember what she had?'

'Let me think . . . I wasn't hungry. I just had some cold cuts . . . Sophie ordered some fish soup that Rose recommended, and then a beef stew.'

'No dessert?'

'No. We had a carafe of Beaujolais. I had a coffee, Sophie didn't want any.'

Maigret went back into the next room and repeated the menu to Delaplanque.

'If she ate at about half past eight, I can already place her death at about eleven at night, because the food was almost entirely digested. I'll be able to tell you more after the chemical analysis, but that'll take a few days.'

'Did you do the paraffin test?'

'Yes, I thought of that. No traces of gunpowder on her hands. You'll get my preliminary report first thing in the morning.'

Maigret returned to sit behind his desk, and arranged in order of size the five or six pipes that were permanently lined up there.

'I've got a few more questions I want to ask you, Ricain, but I'm not sure if it's a good idea to do this today. You're tired out and your nerves are under strain.'

'I'd prefer to get it over with.'

'As you like. To sum up, then, if I've understood you correctly, you've never had a steady job or a regular income?'

'There must be thousands of us like that, I suppose.'

'Who do you still owe money to?'

'All the local traders. Some of them won't serve us any more. I owe five hundred francs to Maki . . .'

'Who's that?'

'A sculptor. He lives in the same building as me. He works in abstracts but now and again, to earn a bit of money, he's willing to make a bust. He got a commission about two weeks ago. He was paid four or five thousand francs and he bought us dinner. Over dessert, I asked him if he could lend me a bit . . .'

'And who else?'

'There are plenty of people!'

'Were you intending to pay them back?'

'One day, I'm sure to be earning a lot of money. Most film directors and famous writers started off like me.'

'Very well, let's change the subject. Were you jealous?'

'Jealous of who?'

'I mean in relation to your wife. I presume there were times when your friends flirted with her?'

Ricain remained silent, looking embarrassed, and gave a shrug.

'I don't think you can understand. You're from a different generation . . . Young people like us don't regard those things as so important.'

'Do you mean that you let her have intimate relations with other men?'

'It's hard to reply to such a crude question.'

'Try, all the same.'

'She posed naked for Maki.'

'And nothing happened?'

'I didn't ask them.'

'What about Monsieur Carus?'

'Carus can have any girl he wants, they all want to be in films or on TV.'

'And he takes advantage?'

'I think so . . .'

'Your wife was trying to get into films, wasn't she?'

'She had a part with a few lines about three months ago.'

'So, you weren't jealous?'

'Not the way you think.'

'Now, you told me that Carus has a mistress . . .'

'Yes, Nora.'

'And is *she* jealous?'

'That's not the same thing. Nora's clever and ambitious. She doesn't care about the cinema. All that interests her is to be Madame Carus and have plenty of money.'

'Did she get on with your wife?'

'As she did with everyone else. Nora looked down on all of us, men and women alike. What are you getting at?'

'Nothing.'

'Are you planning to interview everyone I've been in touch with?'

'Possibly. *Somebody* killed your wife. You tell me you didn't do it, and until I see any evidence to the contrary, I'm inclined to believe you.

'Some person unknown gained entrance to your apartment on Wednesday night, when you had just gone out. This person didn't have a key, which means that your wife let whoever it was in, unsuspectingly.'

Maigret looked seriously at the young man in front of him, who was impatiently trying to get a word in.

'Wait! Which of your friends knew you had a gun?'

'Most of them . . . Probably all of them.'

'Did you carry it on you?'

'No. But if I had a bit of money and invited a few friends round . . . I'd buy some cold meat, salmon, salad things, and everyone would bring their own bottle of wine or whisky . . .'

'And what time would these little parties finish?'

'Pretty late at night. We'd drink a lot. Someone might fall asleep and stay over until the morning . . . I sometimes brought out the pistol as a joke.'

'Was it loaded?'

Ricain did not reply at once and at moments like this it was hard not to suspect him.

'I don't know . . .'

'Look. You're describing to me parties at night, when everyone was more or less drunk. You picked up an automatic weapon, just as a game, and *now* you tell me that you don't know whether it was loaded or not. A little while ago, you said you didn't even know where the safety catch was. You could have killed any one of your friends without meaning to.'

'Yes, that's possible. When you're drunk . . .'

'And were you often drunk, Ricain?'

'Quite often. Not so that I didn't know what I was doing, but yes, I was a heavy drinker, like most of my friends. When you meet up in cafés and nightclubs . . .'

'Where did you keep this pistol?'

'It wasn't locked away. Just in the top drawer of the chest with a lot of old stuff, string, nails, bills, the kind of thing you shove in there.'

'So anyone who'd been to a party at your place could have taken the gun out and used it.'

'Yes.'

'Do you suspect anyone?'

Another hesitation and an evasive expression.

'No.'

'Nobody was truly in love with your wife?'

'Just me.'

Why did he say this in a sarcastic tone?

'In love, but not jealous?'

'I already explained . . .'

'And what about Carus?'

'I told you about him before.'

'Maki?'

'He's a big brute to look at, but he's really as mild as can be, and women scare him.'

'Tell me about the others, the people you run round with, the ones you meet at the Vieux-Pressoir, the ones who would end up at your place when you had a bit of money.'

'There's Gérard Dramin. He's a first assistant. It was with him I worked on a screenplay and I was third assistant on the film.'

'Married?'

'At the moment, he's separated from his wife. Not for the first time. After a few months, they always get back together again.'

'Where does he live?'

'Here and there, always in a hotel room. He boasts he doesn't own anything except a suitcase and what's inside it.'

'Are you getting all this, Janvier?'

'Yes, I'm keeping up, chief.'

'Who else, Ricain?'

'A photographer, Jacques Huguet, who lives in the same building as me, in the central block.'

'Age?'

'Thirty.'

'Married?'

'Twice. And divorced twice. He's got one kid by the first wife and two by the second. She lives on the same floor as him.'

'Does he live alone, then?'

'He's with Jocelyne now, a nice girl, who's seven or eight months pregnant.'

'So that's three women. Does he still see the first two?'

'The wives get on very well.'

'Carry on.'

'Carry on what?'

'With the list of your friends, the regulars at the Vieux-Pressoir.'

'They change, I told you. There's Pierre Louchard . . .'

'And what does he do?'

'He's over forty, he's a homosexual, keeps an antique shop in Rue de Sèvres.'

'What reason does he have to be mixed up with your group?'

'No idea. He's a customer at the Vieux-Pressoir. He follows us around. He doesn't say much, just likes being with us.'

'Do you owe him money?'

'Not much. Three hundred and fifty francs.'

The telephone rang. Maigret picked it up.

'Hello, chief. Lapointe wants a word with you. Shall I put him through?'

'No, I'll come in.'

He returned to the inspectors' office.

'You asked me to call you when we'd finished, chief. Lourtie and I questioned all the neighbours who might have heard anything, especially the women, because most of the men are still at work.

'No one can remember hearing a shot. They're used to hearing noises in the evenings from the Ricains' apartment. Several tenants had complained to the concierge and were thinking of writing to the landlord.

'Once, round about two in the morning, an old woman who was up at her window, because she had a toothache, saw a completely naked girl come out of the apartment and run round the courtyard, followed by a man.

'She isn't the only one who claims they had orgies in the Ricains' place.'

'Did Sophie have callers when her husband wasn't there?'

'You know, chief, the women I talked to weren't too specific. The words that came up most often were: savages, badly brought-up people, no morals. And the concierge was waiting for their lease to expire to ask them to leave, because they're six months behind with the rent, and the owner had decided to get rid of them if they didn't pay up. What shall I do?'

'Stay there till I join you. Keep Lourtie with you; I might need him.'

He returned to his office, where Janvier and Ricain both sat in silence.

'Listen carefully, Ricain. As things stand at present, I don't want the examining magistrate to bring charges against you. But I don't imagine you'd want to go back to sleep in Rue Saint-Charles.'

'I couldn't . . .'

'You don't have any money. I'd rather not let you loose in Paris to go running after a friend for money again . . .'

'What are you going to do with me?'

'Inspector Janvier will take you to a modest hotel near here, on the Ile Saint-Louis. You can order something to eat through room service. On the way, you can pick up a razor, soap and a toothbrush from a chemist's shop.'

The inspector winked at Janvier.

'And I'd prefer it if you didn't leave the hotel. But in any case, I should say that if you did . . .'

'I'd be followed . . . Yes, I get it . . . I'm innocent . . .'

'As you have said.'

'Don't you trust me?'

'It's not my job to trust people. I like to wait and see. Goodnight.'

Once he was alone, Maigret paced round his office for a few minutes, sometimes stopping at the window. Then he picked up the phone and called his wife to say he would not be home for dinner.

Fifteen minutes later, he was back in the Métro and on the way to the Bir-Hakeim station. He knocked at the apartment door and Lapointe opened it.

There were still traces of formalin in the air. Lourtie, sitting in the only armchair in the room, was smoking a small but very strong cigar.

'Want to sit here, chief?'

'No thanks. I suppose you haven't found anything new?'

'Some photos. Here's one where the Ricain couple are on the beach. Another standing by their car.'

Sophie was not at all bad-looking. She had a rather sulky expression, as was the fashion among all the girls, and wore her hair in bouffant style. In the street, she would have been indistinguishable from thousands of others who dressed alike and struck similar poses.

'No wine or alcohol?'

'A bottle in the wardrobe with some dregs of whisky.'

It was an old wardrobe, of no particular style, like the chest and the chairs, but the white matt paint, contrasting with the floor and the red walls, made it look original.

Maigret, hat on head, pipe in mouth, was opening doors

and drawers. Very few clothes. Three dresses in all, cheap and colourful. Some matador pants and polo-neck sweaters.

Next to the bathroom, the kitchenette was hardly more than a cupboard with a gas ring and a small refrigerator. In that he found an opened bottle of mineral water, a quarter-pound of butter, three eggs and a chop sitting in congealed sauce.

Nothing was very clean, neither the clothes, nor the kitchen, nor the bathroom, in which some underclothes were draped.

'Has anyone phoned?'

'Not since we've been here.'

The murder must have been reported in the evening papers, or would be very soon.

'Lourtie, you're to go and get a bite to eat and come back to settle down here as comfortably as possible. OK?'

'Understood, chief. All right if I take a nap?'

As for Maigret and Lapointe, they were setting out on foot in search of the Vieux-Pressoir.

'Have you arrested him, chief?'

'No. Janvier has taken him to the Hotel des Cigognes on the Ile Saint-Louis.'

It wasn't the first time they had lodged there someone they wanted to keep under observation.

'Do you think he did it?'

'He's both clever enough and stupid enough to have done it. Then again . . .'

Maigret searched for words but found none. He had rarely been intrigued by anyone as much as by this François Ricain. At first sight, he was just another ambitious youngster, such as arrive every day in Paris and all capital cities.

Was he heading for failure? He was only twenty-five. Plenty of well-known men were still in their humble beginnings at his age. At times, the inspector was inclined to trust him. Then, next minute, he would be heaving a sigh of discouragement.

'If I was his father . . .'

But what would he do with a son like Francis? Try to calm him down, get him back on the straight and narrow?

He'd have to go and see Ricain's father in Montmartre. Unless he turned up at the Police Judiciaire when he saw the newspapers.

Lapointe, who was walking silently alongside him, was hardly more than twenty-five himself. Maigret made a mental comparison of the two men.

'I think that must be it, chief, across the boulevard by the overhead Métro.'

And indeed they could see a doorway flanked by two wine-press screws made of worm-eaten wood: curtained windows filtered the rosy glow of the lamps lit inside.

It wasn't yet time for aperitifs, let alone dinner, and there were only two people inside the restaurant, a woman perched on a bar stool and sipping a yellowish drink through a straw, and the owner, on the other side of the counter, intent on his newspaper.

The lamps were pink, the bar was supported by wooden screws from a winepress, the massive tables were laid with checked cloths and the walls were clad in dark wooden panelling up to two thirds of their height.

Maigret, who was ahead of Lapointe, frowned when he saw the man reading the newspaper, as if searching his memory.

The owner looked up, but *he* needed no more than a moment to recognize the inspector.

'What a coincidence,' he said, tapping his newspaper, which was hot off the press. 'I've just read that you're leading the investigation . . .'

And turning to the girl at the counter, he said:

'Fernande, let me introduce you to Detective Chief Inspector Maigret in person. Take a seat, inspector. What can I offer you?'

'I didn't know you'd gone into the catering business.'

'Ah, when you're getting on in years . . .'

And it was true that Bob Mandille must have been about the same age as Maigret. He had been well known, back in the old days, when almost every month he would invent a new trick, whether wing-walking, parachuting into Place de la Concorde and landing a few metres away from the obelisk, or jumping from a galloping horse into a racing car.

He had become one of cinema's most famous stuntmen, having failed to become a leading actor. After countless accidents, his body must have been covered with scars.

His figure was still slim and elegant. Only now and then did his movements betray a certain stiffness reminiscent of an automaton. As for his face, it was a little too smooth, and his features too regular, no doubt as a result of plastic surgery.

'A Scotch?'

'A beer.'

'Same for you, young man?'

Lapointe was not at all pleased to be greeted thus.

'As you see, Monsieur Maigret, I called it a day. The insurance companies said I was too old for them to take the risk, they didn't want me any more in films. So I married Rose, and here I am behind a bar. You're looking at my hair? Remember what I looked like when I was scalped by a helicopter rotor, bald as an egg? This is just a wig.'

And he gallantly pulled it off, waving it like a hat.

'You remember Rose, don't you? She sang for years at the Trianon-Lyrique. Rose Delval, she was. Her real name is Rose Vatan, but that didn't work on the posters. So what do you want me to tell you?'

Maigret glanced at the girl who had been addressed as Fernande.

'Don't worry about her, she's part of the furniture. In a couple of hours, she'll be so sozzled she won't be able to walk straight and I'll put her in a taxi.'

'Well, you know Ricain, of course . . .'

'Of course. Cheers! . . . I drink nothing but water, you'll have to excuse me . . . Ricain comes in here for dinner once or twice a week.'

'With his wife?'

'With Sophie, yes, of course. You don't often see Francis without Sophie.'

'When did you last see them together?'

'Let me see . . . What day is it today? . . . Friday . . . They were in on Wednesday night.'

'With friends?'

'There wasn't anyone from their gang in here that night. Except Maki, if I remember correctly . . . I think Maki was eating in his corner.'

'Did they sit at his table with him?'

'No. Francis just pushed open the door, asked me if I'd seen Carus, and I said no, I hadn't seen him for two or three days.'

'What time did they leave?'

'They didn't even come in, they must have eaten somewhere else . . . So what's happening to Francis at the moment? I hope you haven't clapped him in jail.'

'Why do you ask?'

'I just read in the paper that his wife has been shot dead and he's disappeared.'

Maigret smiled. The police in the fifteenth arrondissement, who were not in the know, had misinformed the reporters.

'Who told you about my restaurant?'

'Ricain.'

'So he's not run away?'

'No.'

'Arrested?'

'Not that either. Do you think he would have been capable of killing Sophie?'

'He couldn't kill a fly. If he was ever to kill somebody, it'd be himself.'

'Why?'

'Because there are times when his confidence disappears and he hates himself. Times when he starts drinking. After a few glasses, he's in the depths of despair, sure of being a failure and letting down his wife.'

'Does he pay regularly?'

'He's got quite a lot on the slate. If I was to listen to Rose, I'd have stopped letting him have credit a while back. For Rose, business is business. It's true her work's harder than mine, toiling over the stove all day. That's what she's doing now and will be doing at ten o'clock tonight.'

'Did Ricain come back that evening?'

'Let me think . . . I was busy with a table later on. I felt a draught and turned to the door. It was half-open, and I thought I saw him peering in, looking for someone.'

'Did he find them?'

'No.'

'What time was that?'

'About eleven. You're right to press me on this. Because he *did* come back that night, a third time, a lot later . . . Sometimes when dinner's all over, we stay around to chat with the regulars. It was past midnight on Wednesday when he came in. He stayed near the door, and beckoned me over.'

'Did he know the customers you were with?'

'No, they were old friends of Rose's, theatre people, and Rose had come to join us in her apron. Francis is scared stiff of my wife.

'He asked me if Carus had been in. I told him no. What about Gérard? That's Dramin, now that's a young man who's going to make a name in the cinema. No, he hadn't been in either. Then he blurted out that he needed two thousand francs. I just shook my head. A few dinners on the slate, OK. Perhaps the odd fifty- or hundred-franc note, without Rose seeing, I can do that. But two thousand francs . . .'

'And he didn't tell you why he needed them so urgently?'

'Because he was going to be kicked out of his apartment, and his belongings were going to be auctioned.'

'Was this the first time?'

'No, to tell you the truth. Rose isn't wrong, really: he does touch people for money. But he's not the cynical kind, if you see what I mean. He's in good faith, always sure that something will turn up, that this week or next he'll be signing a big contract. He's so ashamed of asking that you feel ashamed to refuse him.'

'Did he look nervous?'

'You've seen him?'

'Yes, of course.'

'Would you call him nervous or calm?'

'A bundle of nerves.'

'I've never seen him in any other state. Sometimes it's exhausting just to look at him. His hands are clenched, his face is contorted, he takes fright at anything, or else he gets bitter, or up on his high horse. But believe me, inspector, he's a good kid, and I'd be surprised if he didn't amount to something special one day . . .'

'What do you think of Sophie?'

'Well, one shouldn't speak ill of the dead . . . There are plenty of Sophies around, if you know what I mean.'

And with a glance, he nodded over at the girl by the counter who was lost in contemplation of the bottles.

'I wonder what he saw in her. They're all the same, thousands of them, they dress the same way, they all put on the same kind of make-up, they have dirty feet and down-at-heel shoes, they drift about in the morning in trousers that are too tight, and eat salad. Because they want to be models or film stars . . . I ask you!'

'She did get a part once.'

'That would be through Walter, I dare say . . .'

'Walter?'

'Carus. If we knew how many girls have managed to get a part in a film . . .'

'What kind of man is he?'

'If you eat here, you'll probably see him. He's at the same table every other night, and there are always a few spongers taking advantage of his hospitality. He's a film producer. I expect you know how it goes. A man who finds enough money to get a film started; then some more to carry on with it, and after a few months or years, enough to finish it. He's half-English and half-Turkish, odd combination. Good fellow, though, built like a tank, deep voice, always ready to buy a round and after five minutes he's talking to you as if he's known you for ever.'

'Was he the same with Sophie?'

'He's the same with all women, calls them babe, sweetheart, my beauty, depending on the time of day.'

'Do you think he ever slept with her?'

'I'd be surprised if he didn't.'

'And Ricain wasn't jealous?'

'I thought you'd get round to that . . . But in the first place, Carus wasn't the only one. I'd lay a bet the others all did as well. Even me, if I'd wanted to, and I could almost be her granddad. Well, never mind that . . . Rose and me, we had a few words over it . . .

'If you ask Rose, she'll tell you terrible things about him, he's a lazy so-and-so, makes out he's a genius, claims nobody understands him, but he's just a nasty little pimp. That's my wife's view . . .

'It's true that since she spends most of her time in the kitchen, she doesn't know him like I do.

'I tried to make her see Francis didn't know about it . . .'

'Is that what you think?'

The former stuntman had very light blue eyes, like those of a child. In spite of his age and the long experience one could guess at, he had retained a boyish enthusiasm and charm.

'Maybe I'm naive, but I trust that kid . . . There've been days when I've had my doubts, though, days when I've been on the point of agreeing with Rose.

'But I'll stick to my guns on this. He really does love that girl. He loves her enough that she could make him believe anything.

'If you want evidence, look at how she treated him. Some nights, when she'd had a drop too much, she'd say cynically, in front of other people, that he was a failure, a waste of space, with no fire in his belly or anywhere else, for that matter, if you excuse me saying so, and she wondered why she was spending her time with a loser like him.'

'And he took it all?'

'He'd shrink into himself, and you could see sweat on his forehead. But he'd force out a smile and say:

' "Come on, Sophie . . . Bedtime . . . You're tired . . ." '

A door opened at the back of the room. A small, very plump woman emerged, wiping her hands on a large apron.

'Well I never! It's the detective chief inspector!'

And as Maigret was trying to remember where he had met her before, since he had never set foot in the Trianon-Lyrique, she reminded him:

'Twenty-two years ago. In your office. You arrested the man who stole my jewels from my dressing room. I've put on a bit of weight since then, eh? But it was thanks to the jewellery I was able to buy this place. Isn't that so, Bob? So what are you doing here?'

Her husband pointed automatically to the newspaper.

'Sophie's dead.'

'What, our Sophie, Ricain's little wife?'

'Yes.'

'An accident, was it? I'll bet he was driving and—'

'She was murdered.'

'What's this he's saying, Monsieur Maigret?'

'It's the truth.'

'When did it happen?'

'Wednesday night.'

'They didn't eat *here*.'

And Rose's face had lost not only its cheerfulness, which was a kind of trademark, but all cordiality.

'What have you been telling him?'

'I just answered his questions.'

'I bet you told him she was no good. Listen, inspector. Bob's not a bad sort and we rub along pretty well. But when it comes to women, you don't want to listen to him. He thinks they're all sluts, and men are their victims. That poor girl, for instance . . .

'Look at me, Bob. Who was right? Was it him or her that got killed?'

She fell silent, staring at them suspiciously, hands on hips.

'Same again, Bob,' whispered Fernande in a weary voice.

And Mandille, to cut things short with her, poured out a double.

'Did you like Sophie, then, madame?'

'What do you want me to say? She came from the provinces, Concarneau if you please, where her father's a watchmaker. I bet you her mother goes to mass every morning.

'Then she comes to Paris and falls in with this gang of men who all think they're geniuses, whether they work in films or TV. I've been on the stage myself, and that's a lot more difficult. I've sung every song in the repertoire, and I don't give myself airs because of that. But those little idiots . . .'

'Who do you mean exactly?'

'Ricain, for a start, because he thought he was the best of the bunch. If he managed to get an article in a magazine read by two hundred imbeciles, he thought he was going to shake the whole cinema industry to its foundations.

'He took that little girl over. Apparently they really were married. Well then, he could have made enough money to feed her, couldn't he? I don't know what they'd have eaten if friends hadn't paid for them, and if my soft husband hadn't given them credit. How much does he owe you, Bob?'

'Never mind.'

'You see! And me slaving away in the kitchen the whole time.'

She was grumbling now for grumbling's sake, but still eyed her husband with tenderness.

'Do you think she was Carus' mistress?'

'As if he needed her. He had his hands full with Nora.'

'And she's his wife?'

'No, he'd be willing to marry her, but he's already married in London and his wife won't hear of a divorce. As for Nora . . .'

'What's she like?'

'You haven't met her? Well, I'm not going to defend that one. You see, I'm not prejudiced either way . . . But what men see in *her*, I do not know.

'She's at least thirty, and if you saw her without her make-up, it might be nearer forty. She's thin, that's for sure, so skinny you can see her bones sticking through.

'She wears this green and black make-up round her eyes, to give herself a mysterious air supposedly, but it just makes her look like a witch. You can't see her mouth because she puts white greasepaint on her lips, and some greenish-white powder on her cheeks. So that's Nora.

'As for the way she dresses . . . The other day, she turned

75

up in some kind of silver lamé pyjamas so tight she had to come into the kitchen for me to sew up a split in her trousers.'

'And is she in films?'

'You must be joking. She leaves that to the ten-a-penny girls. What she wants is to be the wife of a big international producer, to be Madame Big-Shot one day.'

'You're exaggerating,' Mandille sighed.

'Not as much as you, just now.'

'Nora is intelligent, she's educated, much more educated than Carus, and without her, he probably wouldn't have been so successful.'

Now and then, Maigret would turn towards Lapointe, who was listening in silence, standing still beside the bar and no doubt astonished by what he was hearing and by the atmosphere in the Vieux-Pressoir.

'Will you stay for dinner, Monsieur Maigret? If I have time, if we're not too busy, I'll come over for a chat now and then. I've got some mussels in, so there'll be mouclade this evening. I haven't forgotten I was born in La Rochelle, my mother was a fishmonger, so I know all the good recipes. Have you ever eaten a chaudrée fourassienne?'

Maigret recited:

'A soup made with eels, baby soles and squid.'

'Been down that way often?'

'To La Rochelle, yes, and Fouras.'

'Shall I make you a chaudrée?'

'Yes, please.'

When she had vanished, Maigret grunted:

'Your wife doesn't think the same way as you about these people. If I listened to her, I'd be rushing to arrest François Ricain.'

'I think you'd be making a mistake.'

'Well, who else do you see as a possibility?'

'As the killer? No one. Where was Francis when it happened?'

'Here. And there. He says he was combing the whole of Paris trying to find Carus or someone else who could lend him money. Ah, and he mentioned a nightclub.'

'That'll be the Club Zéro, I'll bet you.'

'Yes, that's right, near Rue Jacob.'

'Carus is often there. Some of my other customers too. One of the latest fashionable clubs. They change every two or three years. Or even in a shorter time, a few months. It's not the first time Francis has been short of cash and gone hunting for someone who'll slip him a couple of thousand in cash.'

'He didn't find Carus anywhere.'

'Did he try the hotel?'

'I expect so.'

'Well, it must mean he was at Enghien. Nora's quite the gambler. Last year, in Cannes, he left her alone in the casino, and when he came back she'd sold her jewels and lost all she got for them. Another beer? You wouldn't prefer some vintage port?'

'No, beer for me. What about you, Lapointe?'

'A port, please,' said the young policeman, blushing.

'Can I use your phone?'

'Back there on the left. Wait, I'll give you some tokens.'

He took a handful from the till and gave them to Maigret without counting them.

'Hello. Inspectors' office? . . . Who's that? . . . Torrence? . . . Anything to report? No one's been asking for me? . . . Moers? . . . I'll call him when I've finished talking to you . . .

'You got a call from Janvier? . . . Still at the Hotel des Cigognes? The kid's sleeping? . . . Good . . . Yes . . . Good. You're going to take over from him? . . . That's fine. Goodnight. But keep an eye on him all the same . . .

'If he wakes up, who knows what ideas he'll get into his head. One moment . . . Can you phone the River Squad? . . . Tomorrow morning they should take some frogmen to the Pont de Bir-Hakeim. A little way upstream, about forty metres, they should find a pistol that's been thrown in from the bank . . . Yes . . . Tell them it's me who wants to know.'

He hung up and dialled the number of the laboratory.

'Moers? . . . You were asking for me? . . . You've found the bullet in the wall? . . . What? . . . Probably the 6.35? . . . Send it off to Gastinne-Renette . . . It's possible that by tomorrow we'll have a gun to show them . . . Fingerprints? . . . Yes, I thought so . . . All over the place . . . Both of them . . . And several other people's . . . Men and women? . . . Doesn't surprise me, they don't seem to have cleaned the place very often . . . Thanks, Moers . . . See you tomorrow.'

François Ricain was lying fast asleep, worn out, in a little room in the Ile Saint-Louis, while Maigret was going to eat a very tasty regional dish, the chaudrée, in the restaurant where the young couple had often met their group of friends.

Coming out of the telephone cabin, he could not help smiling, since Fernande, suddenly waking up again, was talking animatedly to Lapointe, who didn't know where to look.

4.

It was a strange evening, full of sidelong glances, whispers and movements to and fro in the cramped space under the pink lamplight, surrounded by the seductive aromas of the Vieux-Pressoir's cuisine.

Maigret had installed himself near the entrance with Lapointe, in a sort of alcove with a small table for two.

'That's the table where Ricain and Sophie sat, when they weren't with the others,' Bob Mandille had told them.

Lapointe had his back to the room, and sometimes, when Maigret pointed out something interesting to him, he would crane his head round as discreetly as possible.

The chaudrée was delicious, and came accompanied by a modest little wine from the Charentes region not often found for sale, a dry uncompromising wine which is used to make cognac.

The former stuntman was acting the genial host, receiving his customers as if they were guests, greeting them as they arrived. He cracked jokes with them, kissed the ladies' hands, saw them to their tables, and before the waiter took over, gave them the menu.

Almost every time, he would then come towards Maigret.

'An architect and his wife . . . They're here every Friday, sometimes with their son, who's studying law.'

After the architect, two doctors and their wives appeared, also regulars, who took a table for four. One of the doctors was presently called to the telephone and, a few minutes later, he was picking up his bag from the cloakroom and apologizing to his fellow-diners.

Maki, the sculptor, was eating alone in a corner, displaying a healthy appetite and helping himself with his fingers rather more than good manners would allow.

It was half past eight when a dark young man with a sickly face came in and shook the sculptor's hand. He did not sit at the same table, though, but took his place on a banquette, spreading out a typescript in front of him.

'That's Dramin,' Bob announced. 'He usually works while he's eating. This is his latest screenplay and they've already made him rewrite it three or four times.'

Most of the diners knew each other, at least by sight, and greeted one another discreetly from a distance.

From the descriptions he had been given, Maigret immediately recognized Carus and especially Nora, who would not pass unnoticed in any company.

This evening, she was not wearing lamé trousers, but a dress, made from a fabric almost as transparent as cellophane, and so tight-fitting that she appeared to be almost naked.

In her face, under a mask of white make-up like a Pierrot's, her coal-dark eyes were the outstanding feature, outlined not only in black and green but with glitter that sparkled when caught by the lights.

There was something ghostly in her silhouette, her expression, her way of standing, making the contrast even greater with the vitality of Carus, who was a well-built and sturdy man with a healthy, beaming face.

As she followed Bob to their table, Carus went round shaking hands, Maki's, then Dramin's, then those of the remaining doctor and the two wives.

When he had sat down in turn, Bob leaned over to whisper a few words to him, and the producer searched the room for Maigret, his eyes alighting on him with curiosity. It looked as if he was about to stand up and come over to shake hands with the inspector too, but he began by examining the menu he had been handed, and discussing his choice with Nora.

When Mandille returned to Maigret's corner, the latter expressed surprise.

'I thought the gang would sit round the same table.'

'They do now and then. But other evenings, they each stay in their own corner. They might meet up for coffee afterwards. Some nights they sit down all together. Our regulars feel at home here. We have hardly any passers-by dropping in and we like it that way.'

'Do they all know the news?'

'They will have seen the paper or heard the radio bulletin, of course.'

'What are they saying?'

'Not a word. They're all shocked. Your presence here must be worrying for them . . . What will you have after the chaudrée? My wife recommends the leg of lamb, authentic saltmarsh.'

'Lamb for you, Lapointe? Yes, for us both.'

'And a carafe of red? I've got a nice little Bordeaux.'

Through the curtains, they could see the lights on the boulevard, people walking past quickly or slowly, sometimes a couple who stopped to embrace or exchange loving looks.

Dramin, as Bob had told them, was eating while reading through the typescript, taking a pencil from his pocket from time to time to correct something. He was the only one of Ricain's friends not to look as if he was concerned by the presence of the policemen.

He wore a dark, off-the-peg suit and an ordinary tie. He could have been taken for an accountant or a bank teller.

'Carus is wondering whether he will come over and talk to me or not,' Maigret announced, as he observed the couple. 'I don't know what advice Nora is giving him with that stern expression, but he doesn't agree.'

He imagined how, on other nights, François Ricain and Sophie would have come in, looked around for their friends, wondering if they would be invited to a table or whether they would be eating alone in their corner. They would surely have seemed like poor relations.

'Are you going to question them, chief?'

'Not just now. After the leg of lamb.'

It was very warm in the restaurant. The doctor who had been called away to a patient's bedside was already back, and it could be guessed from his gestures that he was complaining at having been disturbed to no purpose.

Where had Fernande gone, the tall girl, worse the wear for drink, who had been clinging to the bar? Bob must have got rid of her. He was now chatting to three or four male customers who had taken her place. They were talking to each other with familiarity and good humour.

'The ghost-woman is giving her husband instructions.'

Indeed, she was speaking to him guardedly, not taking her eyes off Maigret, and apparently giving Carus advice. But what kind of advice?

'He's still hesitating. He's dying to come over here, but she's holding him back. I think I'll take myself across.'

Maigret heaved himself to his feet after patting his lips with his napkin, and made his way through the tables. The couple watched him approach, Nora impassively, Carus with visible satisfaction.

'I'm not disturbing you?'

The film producer stood up, wiped his lips in turn and held out his hand.

'Walter Carus . . . My wife . . .'

'Detective Chief Inspector Maigret.'

'I know. Please do sit down. Can I offer you a glass of champagne? It's the only thing my wife drinks, and I don't blame her. Joseph! A glass for the inspector.'

'Please don't interrupt your meal.'

'No point pretending I don't know why you are here. I heard the news just now on the radio, when I went back to my hotel for a shower and change of clothes.'

'Did you know the Ricain couple well?'

'Quite well . . . Here we all know each other. He more or less worked for me, in the sense that I had some money invested in the film he was employed on.'

'Did his wife not also get a bit part in another of your films?'

'I'd forgotten that. She was more like an extra.'

'Did she want to work in films?'

'Not seriously. I don't think so. But most girls that age like to see themselves up on the screen.'

'Was she talented at all?'

Maigret had the impression that Nora had given a little kick to Carus' ankle as a warning.

'I must say I really don't know. I don't even think she'd been given a screen test.'

'What about Ricain?'

'Are you asking me if he's talented?'

'What sort of man is he professionally?'

'What would you say, Nora?'

And she let fall in an icy tone:

'Nothing.'

This had the effect of being a conversation stopper and Carus hastened to explain.

'Don't be surprised. Nora is something of a medium. She possesses a sort of fluid that makes her immediately able to make contact with some people, but with others it works the other way. Believe it or not, this fluid – sorry that's the only word I can find for it – has often helped me in business, even on the Stock Exchange.'

The foot was hard at work under the table once more.

'With Francis, she never really found it possible to make contact. Personally I find him intelligent and gifted, and I'd be willing to bet he has a successful career in front of him.

'Take Dramin, over there, for instance, deep in his screenplay. He's a serious young fellow who does his work as efficiently as possible. I've read some excellent dialogues he's written. But still, unless I'm completely mistaken, he'll never be a great director. He needs someone not only to tell him what to do, but to add that indispensable spark.'

He was delighted with the word he had found.

'Yes, the spark! That's what's lacking most of the time, and it's essential whether you're in cinema or television. Hundreds of professionals can turn out a good piece of work, a solidly constructed plot, some dialogue that flows along nicely. But almost always something's missing, and the result is grey and boring. The spark, you understand?

'Well, you can't count on Francis to provide you with something solid – his ideas are often fantastical. He's described to me God knows how many scenarios that would completely ruin me. But on the other hand, from time to time, he's got that spark.'

'In what respect?'

Carus scratched his nose, comically.

'Now that is the question. You're talking like Nora. One evening, at the end of dinner, he will launch into something with such conviction and passion that you feel sure you're in the presence of a genius. Then next day, you realize that what he said didn't stand up. He's young. Things will settle down . . .'

'Is he working for you at the moment?'

'Apart from his reviews, remarkable critical articles, though a bit too ferocious, he doesn't work for anyone in particular. He's bubbling with plans, prepares several film outlines at a time without finishing any of them.'

'Does he ask you for advances?'

The feet were continuing their silent conversation under the table.

'Well, you see, inspector, our profession's not like other spheres. We're always on the lookout for talent, whether in performers, writers or directors. It's not profitable to keep hiring the same well-known director who will keep on turning out the same old film for you, and as for the stars, well, you need new faces.

'So we have to take a chance on a certain number of promising youngsters. A very modest chance, or we'd soon be ruined. A thousand francs here and there, a screen test, a little encouragement . . .'

'So, if you were quite willing to lend Ricain money, it was because you thought it would pay off one day?'

'Not that I was holding my breath.'

'And Sophie?'

'I wasn't involved in her career.'

'But she was hoping to become a star?'

'Don't put words in my mouth. She was always in her husband's company and didn't say much. I think she was shy.'

An ironic smile appeared on Nora's pale lips.

'My wife thinks differently, and since I'm more confident in her judgement than my own, you shouldn't attach much importance to my opinion.'

'What was the relationship like between Francis and Sophie?'

'What do you mean?'

He was pretending to be surprised.

'Did they seem attached to each other?'

'You rarely saw one without the other, and I can't recall them quarrelling in my presence.'

The smile had returned, enigmatically, to Nora's lips.

'Perhaps she was getting a little impatient.'

'In what way?'

'He believed in his star, his future, a brilliant future just round the corner. I suppose that when she married him, she imagined she was going to be the wife of a famous man. Famous and rich. But after three years, they were still stony broke, and she had hardly a dress to put on her back.'

'Did she blame him for it?'

'Not in company, to my knowledge.'

'Did she have lovers?'

Nora turned towards Carus with the air of waiting with curiosity for his reply.

'Ah now, you're asking me a question that . . .'

'Why don't you tell the truth?'

For the first time, she was no longer content to make signs under the table, but had opened her mouth to speak.

'My wife is referring to a trivial incident . . .'

Nora, bitingly, let fall:

'That depends for whom.'

'One night, when we had all had a lot to drink . . .'

'And this was where?'

'At the Hotel Raphaël. We'd been here. Maki was with us, Dramin, and a photographer, Huguet, who works for an advertising company. I think Bob had come along too.

'In the hotel, I had room service bring us champagne and whisky. Later, I went to the bathroom, which meant going through our bedroom, where only the bedside lamps were lit.

'I found Sophie lying on one of the beds. Thinking she was unwell, I leaned over her . . .'

Nora's smile was becoming more and more sarcastic.

'She was crying. I had a hard time getting a word out of her. She said she was in despair, wanted to kill herself.'

'And what were you doing when I found the pair of you?'

'I did automatically take her in my arms, it's true, but to comfort her, as one would a child.'

'I asked you whether she had lovers. I wasn't thinking of you in particular.'

'She posed naked for Maki, but I'm sure Maki would never lay a finger on a friend's wife.'

'Was Ricain jealous?'

'You're asking me too much, Monsieur Maigret . . . Your good health! . . . It all depends what you mean by jealousy. He wouldn't have wanted to lose his influence with her, or see another man become more important to her than he was. In that sense, he was jealous of his friends as well. If, for instance, I asked Dramin to come over to our table for coffee without inviting him too, he would sulk for a week.'

'I think I understand.'

'You aren't having a dessert?'

'No, I don't often have one.'

'Nora doesn't either. Bob, what do you advise for dessert?'

'Crêpe flambée with maraschino?'

Carus looked down comically at his stomach and protruding belly.

'Why not? What the hell! OK, a crêpe, then. Two or three, in fact. But with Armagnac rather than maraschino.'

All this time, poor Lapointe was twiddling his thumbs at his table, his back to the room. Maki was picking his teeth with a matchstick, and no doubt wondering whether it would presently be his turn to find the inspector sitting down in front of him.

The doctors' table was the most animated, and one of the women from time to time let out a shrill laugh that made Nora wince.

Rose left her stove for a moment to come round the tables, wiping her hand on her apron before holding it out. She too, like the doctors, was in a good mood, which the news of Sophie's death did not seem to have affected.

'Well, Walter, you old rogue? How come we haven't seen you since Wednesday?'

'I had to catch a plane to Frankfurt to see a business associate and then I went on to London.'

'And did you go with him, my dear?'

'Not this time. I had a fitting session.'

'And you're not afraid of letting him gad about on his own?'

She moved away with a laugh, stopping at one customer, then another. On a table alongside the Caruses, Bob was flambéing the crêpes.

'So now I understand why Ricain looked for you in vain half the night,' the former stuntman said to Carus.

'Why was he looking for me?'

'The inspector told me just now. He urgently needed two thousand francs. On Wednesday he came in here and was asking for you.'

'My plane left at five o'clock.'

'He came back twice. He wanted me to lend it to him, but that was too much money for me. He went off to the club.'

'Why did he need two thousand francs?'

'The landlord was threatening to throw them out.'

Carus turned to Maigret.

'Is this true?'

'It's what he told me.'

'Have you arrested him?'

'No, why?'

'I don't know. Yes, that was a stupid question.'

'Do *you* think he could have killed Sophie?'

The feet, always the feet! Their language could be followed under the table, while Nora's face gave nothing away.

'I can't see him killing anyone. What was the weapon? The newspaper didn't say. Or the radio.'

'An automatic.'

'Francis would never have had a firearm.'

'Yes, he did,' Nora's dry, clipped voice interrupted. 'You've seen it. And that night at his place, you were frightened, frankly. He'd drunk a lot, and he was acting out a hold-up scene.

'He put one of Sophie's stockings over his head, and ordered us to stand against the wall with our hands up. We all obeyed, since it was a game.

'You were the only one who was worried and asked if the gun was loaded.'

'You're right. It comes back to me now. I didn't pay much attention at the time. I'd had a few drinks myself.'

'In the end he put the gun back into a drawer in the chest.'

'Who was there that night?' Maigret asked.

'All the gang . . . Maki, Dramin, Pochon. Dramin came with a girl I'd never seen and I can't remember much about her. She was ill, and spent almost an hour in the bathroom.'

'Jacques was there too.'

'With his new woman, yes. She's already pregnant.'

'Did anyone know that last year, probably, Sophie was pregnant too?'

Why did Nora turn abruptly towards Carus? He looked at her in surprise.

'Did you know?'

'No. If she had a child . . .'

'No, she didn't,' Maigret clarified. 'She got rid of it some-time between the third and fourth month.'

'We didn't realize . . .'

Maki in his corner was coughing significantly as if to get Maigret to move on. He had long finished eating and was getting impatient.

'We've told you all we know, inspector. If you need to see me again, call in at my office.'

And did he really wink as he took a card from his wallet and handed it over?

Maigret had the feeling that Carus had plenty more to

say, but that Nora's presence was preventing him from doing so.

Back in his corner, Maigret was finally packing a pipe when Lapointe told him with a slight smile:

'He's still hesitating. But he'll soon be over.'

He meant Maki. With his back to the room, Lapointe could not survey it, so had spent his time observing the sculptor, the only one in his field of vision.

'At first, when you sat down at the Caruses' table, he frowned, then he shrugged his shoulders. He had a carafe of red wine on the table. Less than five minutes later, he'd finished it and was making signs to the waiter to bring him another.

'He didn't miss one of your movements or expressions. You'd have thought he was trying to lip-read what you were all saying. He soon got impatient. At one point, he called the owner over and whispered something. They both looked towards you.

'Then he half got up, after checking his watch. I thought he was going to leave, but he ordered an Armagnac and they brought him a shot glass. Here he comes now.'

Lapointe was not mistaken. Maki, vexed no doubt because Maigret was not troubling to see him, had decided to come over himself. He remained standing, a huge man, in front of the two policemen.

'Excuse me,' he said in a low voice, putting one hand to his temple in a kind of greeting. 'I wanted to warn you that I'm about to leave.'

Maigret lit his pipe with a series of little puffs.

'Sit down, Monsieur Maki. Is that your real name?'

Sitting down heavily, the man muttered:

'No, of course not. My name's Lecoeur. But that wouldn't do for a sculptor, nobody would have taken me seriously.'

'You knew I wanted to speak to you?'

'Well, since I'm a pal of Francis . . .'

'How did you hear the news?'

'When I got here. I hadn't read the evening paper, and I never listen to the radio.'

'And did it give you a shock?'

'I feel sorry for Francis.'

'Not Sophie?'

He was not drunk, but his cheeks were flushed and his gestures a little too deliberate.

'Sophie was a slut.'

He looked at them each in turn, as if challenging them to contradict him.

'What did Monsieur Carus tell you?'

He emphasized 'monsieur' in an ironic way, as clowns do.

'He doesn't know anything, naturally. What about you?'

'What kind of thing should I know?'

'When did you see Francis Ricain and his wife for the last time?'

'I saw him on Wednesday.'

'Without her?'

'He was alone.'

'What time was that?'

'About half past ten. He talked to me before going to find Bob. I'd finished my dinner, I was just sipping my Armagnac.'

'And what did he say to you?'

'He asked me if I knew where he might find Carus. I should say that I work for that gentleman too. Well, in a way . . . When he needed some kind of sculpture for a ridiculous film, a horror film, I provided him with something appropriate.'

'Did he pay you?'

'Half the agreed price. I'm still waiting for the other half.'

'And did Francis tell you why he was looking for Carus?'

'You know very well why. He needed two thousand smackers. I didn't have that kind of money. I bought him a drink and he left.'

'And you haven't seen him since?'

'Neither him, nor her. What did that Nora tell you?'

'Nothing much. She didn't seem particularly fond of Sophie.'

'She isn't fond of anyone . . . No wonder she's flat-chested . . . I beg your pardon, that wasn't very witty. But I can't stand her. Or him either, with his smiles and handshakes . . . At first sight, they look badly matched, him all honey, her all vinegar, but deep down, they're the same.

'If someone can be useful to them, they squeeze them till the pips squeak, then chuck them away like orange peel.'

'Is that what happened to you?'

'What did they tell you about Francis? You didn't answer my question.'

'Carus appears to think highly of him.'

'What about her?'

'She doesn't like him.'

'Did they talk about Sophie?'

'They told me some story about a bedroom, one night at the Hotel Raphaël, when everyone was drunk.'

'I was there.'

'And apparently nothing happened between him and Sophie.'

'Like hell it didn't!'

'You saw them?'

'I went through the bedroom twice to go to the toilet, without them seeing me. She tried it on with me too. She wanted me to make a sculpture of her, but I do abstracts. I ended up agreeing, to stop her pestering me.'

'Were you her lover?'

'I had to sleep with her, out of good manners. She'd have been angry with me if I hadn't. I wasn't too proud of myself, because of Francis. He didn't deserve to marry a tramp.'

'Did she talk to you about her idea of suicide, as well?'

'Suicide? That girl? In the first place, when a woman talks about it you can be sure she'll never do it. She was putting on an act. With everyone. And with a different part for everyone else to play.'

'Did Francis know?'

Maigret was starting to say Francis like the others, as if he was gradually becoming one of Ricain's group of friends.

'If you want my opinion, he suspected something. He turned a blind eye, but he was seething underneath. Did he really love her? Sometimes I wonder. He made it look that way. He had taken charge of her and didn't want to let her down. She must have made him believe that she'd kill herself if he left her.'

'Do you think he's talented?'

'It's more than talent. Of all of us, he's the only one who'll do something really important. I'm not bad in my way, but I know my limits. Him, when he puts his mind to it one day . . .'

'Thank you, Monsieur Maki.'

'Just Maki. It's a name that doesn't go with monsieur.'

'Goodnight, Maki.'

'Goodnight, inspector. And this is one of your men? Goodnight to you too.'

He walked off with heavy steps, after nodding farewell to Bob.

Maigret mopped his brow.

'There's still Dramin left, the one with his nose in his screenplay. But I've had enough for tonight.'

He looked round for the waiter and called for the bill. Mandille hurried up.

'Allow me to offer you . . .'

'No, impossible,' said Maigret with a sigh.

'Will you at least accept a glass of special Armagnac?'

They could not refuse.

'Did you get the information you wanted?'

'I'm gradually getting to know the group.'

'They're not all here tonight. And the atmosphere is

different every day. Some evenings it's jolly, almost riotous. You didn't speak to Gérard.'

He pointed at Dramin, who was heading for the door, his papers in his hand.

'Hey, Gérard. Let me introduce Detective Chief Inspector Maigret and one of his inspectors. Will you have a drink with us?'

Apparently very short-sighted, the other man wore thick spectacles and poked his head forwards.

'Pleased to meet you. I beg your pardon. I've got some work to finish. But tell me, has Francis been arrested?'

'No. Why?'

'I don't know. Excuse me.'

He took down his hat from the hook and opened the door, disappearing down the road.

'Don't pay too much attention, He's always like that. I think it's a pose, a way of making himself seem important. He's playing the absent-minded genius, the lone wolf. Perhaps he's annoyed that you didn't approach him. I'm pretty sure he didn't read a line all evening.'

'Your very good health!' murmured Maigret. 'And now, as far as I'm concerned, I need to get home to bed . . .'

Nevertheless he called in, with Lapointe, at Rue Saint-Charles and knocked at the Ricains' door. Lourtie opened it. He had taken his jacket off and his hair was tousled after sleeping in the armchair. The room was lit only by a faint nightlight and a smell of disinfectant lingered in the air.

'Nobody came?'

'Two journalists. I didn't tell them anything, except that they should inquire at Quai des Orfèvres.'

'No phone calls?'

'Someone called twice.'

'Who?'

'I don't know. I heard it ring, picked up and said "Hello". I could hear breathing at the other end of the line, but they didn't speak, and hung up on me after a bit.'

'Both times?'

'Yes, both times.'

'When was this?'

'The first call was at about ten past eight, and the second just a few moments ago.'

Within minutes, Maigret was dozing off in the small black police car taking him home.

'I'm exhausted,' he admitted to his wife as he started to undress.

'I hope you had a good dinner.'

'Too good. I must take you to that restaurant sometime. It's run by a former operetta singer who's taken up cooking. She made a dish called a chaudrée that was simply . . .'

'What time in the morning?'

'Seven.'

'So early?'

Yes indeed, so early, since it was suddenly seven o'clock, without any transition. Maigret did not even feel he had been asleep when the smell of coffee reached him, as his wife tapped his shoulder before drawing the curtains.

The sun shone bright and warm. It was wonderful to open the window as soon as he woke up and hear the sparrows cheeping.

'I suppose I shouldn't count on you at midday?'

'No, I probably won't have time to get home for lunch. This is a strange case. Strange people. I'm in the world of cinema and, just like at the cinema, it all started with a stunt, the theft of my wallet.'

'Do you think it was him that killed her?'

Madame Maigret, who knew about the case only through the newspapers and the radio, immediately regretted her question.

'I'm sorry . . .'

'I wouldn't know what to answer, anyway.'

'You're not taking your lightweight coat?'

'No. The weather's the same as yesterday, and I wasn't cold even coming back at night.'

He didn't wait for the bus, but hailed a taxi to take him to the Ile Saint-Louis. Opposite the Hotel des Cigognes was a little café with a zinc counter surrounded by piles of logs and sacks of coal. Torrence, his face sagging with fatigue, was drinking a coffee there when Maigret arrived.

'How was the night?'

'As usual with a surveillance job. Nothing happened, except that I know now what time they all put their lights out. Must be someone ill on the fourth floor, right-hand side, because there was a light in the window until six a.m.

'Your Ricain didn't go out. Some of the guests came back. A taxi brought a couple of travelling salesmen. A dog attached itself to me and followed me almost all night as I walked up and down. And that's all.'

'You can go home to bed.'

'What about my report?'

'You can write it up tomorrow.'

Maigret went inside the hotel. He had known the owner for thirty years. It was a modest establishment, frequented almost entirely by regulars, largely from eastern France, since the proprietor was himself Alsatian.

'Has my guest woken up?'

'He rang ten minutes ago, to ask if someone could bring him a cup of coffee and some croissants. They've just taken it all up.'

'What did he eat last night?'

'Nothing. He must have gone straight off to sleep, because when we knocked at his door at seven, there was no reply. Who is he? An important witness? A suspect . . .?'

There was no lift. Maigret climbed the four floors on foot, reached the landing out of breath, and waited a moment standing there before knocking on the door of Room 43.

'Who is it?'

'Maigret.'

'Come in.'

Pushing his tray away from him on the coverlet, Francis sat up straighter in bed, thin and bare-chested, a bluish shadow on his chin, his eyes feverish. He was still holding a croissant in his hand.

'Excuse me for not getting up, but I don't have any pyjamas.'

'Did you sleep well?'

'As if I'd been knocked out. I slept so soundly my head's still ringing. What time is it?'

'A quarter past eight.'

The bedroom, small and meagrely furnished, looked out on to a courtyard and rooftops. Through the open window, voices from the nearby houses could be heard as well as cries of children in a school playground.

'Have you found anything out?'

'I had dinner at the Vieux-Pressoir.'

Ricain observed him keenly, already on the defensive, and it was visible that he suspected everyone of lying to him.

'Were they there?'

'The Caruses were there.'

'What did he say?'

'He swears you're some kind of genius.'

'I dare say Nora took care to tell him that I'm just an idiot.'

'More or less. She certainly doesn't like you as much as he does.'

'And she liked Sophie even less!'

'Maki was there too.'

'Was he drunk?'

'Just at the end of the evening, he got a bit unsteady.'

'He's a good man.'

'He is also sure that one day you'll be somebody.'

'Meaning that I'm a nobody right now.'

He didn't finish his croissant. It was as though Maigret's arrival had taken away his appetite.

'What do they think about what happened? That I killed Sophie?'

'To tell the truth, no one believes you're guilty. But

some of them supposed that the police would see things differently, so they all asked me if you were under arrest.'

'What did you tell them?'

'The truth.'

'Which is?'

'That you are free.'

'You think that's really the truth? What am I doing here, then? Admit it, you've had a man on duty all night outside the hotel.'

'Did you see him?'

'No, but I know that's how things work. What's going to happen to me now?'

Maigret was asking himself the same question. He had no wish to let Ricain run about freely all over Paris, but on the other hand he had insufficient cause to arrest him.

'First of all, I'll ask you to come with me to Quai des Orfèvres.'

'Again?'

'I might have a few questions to ask you. And, by then, the divers from the River Squad may have found your pistol.'

'Whether they find it or not, what would that change?'

'You've got a razor and soap here. There's a shower room along the corridor. I'll wait for you downstairs or outside.'

A new day was starting, as bright and mild as the previous two, but it was too soon to know how it would turn out.

François Ricain intrigued Maigret, and the opinions he had collected the night before inclined the inspector to take a favourable view of him.

Ricain was at all events an unusual young man, and Carus had been impressed by his potential. But then, didn't Carus get enthusiastic every time an artist was introduced to him, only to drop him or her a few months or weeks later?

Maigret needed to go and see him in his office, where the producer had given him an enigmatic rendezvous. He had something to tell him, something he didn't want to say in front of Nora. She had sensed that and the inspector wondered whether Carus would be at Rue de Bassano that morning, or whether his mistress might have prevented him going there.

He had so far only skimmed the surface of this small world: thousands of similar circles, tens of thousands even, must exist in Paris, made up of friends, relations, colleagues, lovers and mistresses, fellow-regulars of a café or restaurant, circles that form, grow close for a while, then break up to form other more or less parallel little worlds.

What was the name of the photographer who had been married twice, with children from both wives, and who had now got his new mistress pregnant?

He was still at the stage of mixing up some of their names and situations. And yet Sophie's murder had been committed by someone who knew the couple well – or perhaps only the young woman. Otherwise, she wouldn't have opened the door.

Unless someone else had a key?

He was pacing up and down, as Torrence had been doing all night long, but Maigret had the good fortune to be walking in the sunshine. The street was busy with housewives who turned round to look at this gentleman coming and going, hands behind his back, like a school-master in the playground. Yes, there were plenty more questions to ask Francis. And no doubt, just like yesterday, he would be faced with a twitchy creature, bridling every now and then before calming down, suspicious, impa-tient, prone to sudden outbursts.

'Here I am. I'm ready.'

Maigret pointed to the coal and wood merchant's café.

'You wouldn't like a drink of something?'

'No thanks.'

Pity, since Maigret would willingly have started this nice spring day with a little glass of white wine.

5.

It was a tough moment to get through. In almost all his investigations, Maigret experienced this more or less long period of uncertainty, in the course of which, his colleagues whispered, he seemed to be ruminating.

During the first phase of a case, that is when he was suddenly faced with a new milieu and people about whom he knew nothing, it was as if he was breathing in the life around him, absorbing it like a sponge.

That was what he had done the previous evening in the Vieux-Pressoir, his memory registering, without consciously doing so, the smallest details of the atmosphere, the gestures and facial expressions of everyone there.

If he hadn't been feeling so tired, he would have gone on to Club Zéro, which was frequented by some members of the little gang.

And now, he had taken in a huge number of impressions, a jumble of images, of sentences spoken, of words that might or might not mean something, of surprised expressions, but he was still undecided what he would do with it all.

His close colleagues knew that it was best not to ask him any questions, or even to look at him inquiringly, since he would very likely turn crotchety.

As he had been expecting, a note on his desk asked him to call the examining magistrate Camus.

'Hello. Maigret here.'

He had only occasionally worked with this magistrate, whom he regarded neither as a complete pain in the neck, nor among those who wisely allowed the police to get on with their job.

'If I asked you to call me, it was because I've had a call myself from the public prosecutor. He's impatient to know what stage the investigation has reached.'

Maigret almost muttered 'Nowhere'.

Which was true. A crime isn't like an algebra problem. It has to do with human beings about whom nothing was known yesterday, who were just passers-by like anyone else. Then suddenly, every one of their gestures, every word they speak, takes on significance and their whole life is examined with a fine-tooth comb.

'The investigation is ongoing,' he preferred to say. 'Within an hour or so, we shall probably have the murder weapon. The police divers are looking for it in the Seine.'

'What have you done with the husband?'

'He's here, in the icebox.'

He checked himself, since this was a term that could be understood only by the inspectors in his squad. When they did not know what to do with a witness but wanted to keep him in sight, or when they had a suspect not yet ready to be charged, they put him in 'the icebox'.

They would say, as they took the individual concerned into the glass-panelled waiting room, looking on to the long corridor:

'Wait here for a moment.'

There were people there permanently: anxious women,

some crying and dabbing their eyes with handkerchiefs, small-time crooks trying to brazen it out, and now and then solid citizens who remained patiently waiting, looking at the pale-green painted walls, and wondering if the authorities had forgotten their existence.

An hour or two in the icebox was generally enough to make people ready to talk. Even witnesses determined not to say a word became easier to deal with.

It sometimes happened that they were 'forgotten' for half a day, so they kept looking at the door, half-rising every time the usher approached, hoping that it was at last their turn.

They would see the inspectors go off at midday, and pluck up their courage to go and ask Joseph:

'Are you sure the chief knows I'm here?'

'He's still in a meeting.'

For want of any other possibility, Maigret had put Ricain in the icebox.

He translated for the benefit of the examining magistrate:

'He's in the waiting room. I'll question him again when I have more information.'

'What's your impression of him? Guilty?'

Another question the magistrate would not have asked if he had worked for longer with Maigret.

'I don't have any impression yet.'

This was true. He always waited as long as possible before forming an opinion. And even then he did not really *form* the opinion. He kept an open mind until the moment when something became evident to him, or until the interviewee cracked.

'Do you think this is going to take long?'

'I hope not.'

'Have we ruled out the possibility that it is money-related, a robbery gone wrong?'

As if all crimes weren't money-related. In the Palais de Justice and the Police Judiciaire, people did not have the same view of human character or speak the same language.

It was difficult to imagine that some unknown individual looking for money might have turned up after ten at night in Rue Saint-Charles, and that Sophie Ricain, already in her nightclothes, would have let him or her into the flat without suspecting anything.

Either the murderer had a key, or it was someone whom she knew and trusted. Especially if the killer had had to open the drawer in the chest in her presence, to take the gun out.

'Could you kindly keep me informed? Don't make me wait too long. The prosecutor's office is getting impatient.'

Of course! The prosecutor's office is always impatient. These gentlemen who sit comfortably in their offices and whose only acquaintance with crime is through legal papers and statistics. A phone call from the minister's office has them shaking in their shoes.

'Why hasn't anyone been arrested yet?'

The minister, in turn, is driven by the impatience of the newspapers. For the press, a good crime is one that delivers a juicy development every day. If the reader is left too long without news, he'll forget all about the case. One scandal displaces another, and you lose your chance for a good headline.

'Very well, sir . . . Yes, sir . . . I'll call you back.'

He winked at Janvier.

'Go into the corridor now and then to see what he's doing. He's the kind of man who might throw a fit, or try to force my door.'

He nevertheless went through his mail, and attended the morning briefing, the daily occasion to meet his colleagues and discuss current cases dispassionately.

'Nothing to report, Maigret?'

'Nothing to report, chief.'

Here, people didn't insist. They were all professionals who knew their job.

When Maigret returned to his office a little before ten, the River Squad was calling him.

'You've found the gun?'

'We got lucky, the current's quite weak at the moment, and the Seine was dredged at this point last autumn. My men found it almost at once, about forty metres upstream from the bridge, and ten metres from the left bank. A 6.35 automatic, made in Belgium. The magazine still had five rounds in it.'

'Can you send it to Gastinne-Renette, please?'

And to Janvier:

'Can you look after this? He's already been sent the bullet.'

'Right, chief.'

Maigret almost telephoned to Rue de Bassano, then decided not to give advance notice, and headed for the main staircase, avoiding turning towards the waiting room.

His departure would not go unnoticed by Ricain, who would no doubt be wondering where he was off to. On his way, he met young Lapointe just arriving, so instead of taking a taxi as he had intended, he asked Lapointe to drive to the building where Carus had his offices.

He took the time to look at the brass plates under the archway, noting that there was a firm connected to the cinema on virtually every floor. The one that interested him was called Carossoc and its premises were on the mezzanine landing.

'Shall I come up with you?'

'Yes, I'd prefer that.'

Not only was it his method, but it was also recommended in the rulebook for officers of the Police Judiciaire.

The entry hall was rather dark, its only window giving on to the courtyard where a chauffeur could be seen polishing a Rolls-Royce. A red-headed secretary was sitting in front of the switchboard.

'Monsieur Carus, please.'

'I don't know if he's arrived yet.'

As if anybody could reach the other offices without walking past her!

'Who shall I say? You have an appointment?'

'Detective Chief Inspector Maigret.'

She stood up and made as if to take them to the waiting room, putting them in an icebox too.

'No thanks, we'll wait here.'

Visibly, she was not best pleased at this. Instead of telephoning through to her boss, she opened a padded door and left the room for three or four minutes.

The first person to emerge was not the secretary but Carus in person, wearing a light grey pinstripe suit and freshly shaved, spreading a smell of lavender around him.

He had clearly just come from his barber's, and had no doubt also had a face massage, being the kind of man who probably spent a good half-hour every morning in the swivel chair.

'My dear friend, how are you?'

He extended a cordial hand to the dear friend, of whose existence he had been unaware at six the previous evening.

'Do come in. And you too, young man. I suppose this is one of your colleagues?'

'Inspector Lapointe.'

'You may leave us, mademoiselle. If anyone asks, I'm not here, and I won't take any call, unless it's from New York.'

He explained with a smile:

'I hate being interrupted by phone calls.'

There were nevertheless three telephones on his desk. The room was immense, the walls covered in padded beige leather like the armchairs, while the deep-pile carpet was a pastel chestnut colour.

As for the huge rosewood desk, it was laden with enough files to keep a dozen secretaries employed.

'Do sit down. What can I offer you?'

He headed for a low sideboard which turned out to be a well-stocked bar.

'It's a little early for an aperitif, but I imagine you are a connoisseur of beer. And so am I. I have some excellent stuff here. I get it delivered directly from Munich.'

He was being more amiable than the night before, perhaps because he had no need to worry about Nora's reactions.

'Yesterday, you took me a bit by surprise . . . When I went out to have dinner, as I often do, at my old friend Bob's place, I wasn't expecting to meet you. I'd had two or three whiskies beforehand, and what with the champagne . . . Not that I was drunk. I never am. But this morning, I only have a very vague memory of what we talked about. My wife told me off for talking too much and too emotionally. Your good health, inspector! . . . I hope that wasn't the impression I gave you.'

'You seem to consider François Ricain as a worthwhile young man, who has every chance of becoming a leading film director.'

'I may have said that, yes. I make a habit of trusting young people and, of course, I often make a show of my enthusiasm.'

'But you don't think the same thing this morning?'

'Oh yes, I do. Yes indeed. More or less . . . The kid's a bit disorganized. A bit anarchic. Half the time he's overconfident and the other half he's completely unsure of himself.'

'If I remember correctly what you said, the Ricains' marriage was, in your view, quite a close one.'

Carus had seated himself in one of the leather armchairs, crossing his legs, a glass in one hand, a cigar in the other.

'Did I say that?'

He suddenly decided to stand up, put the glass down

on a surface, puffed on the cigar a few times, and paced across the carpet.

'Look here, detective chief inspector, I was hoping you'd come round this morning.'

'That's what I understood.'

'Nora is an exceptional woman. Although she never sets foot in the office, I could sincerely say she is my best collaborator.'

'You mentioned her gift as a medium . . .'

He waved his hand as if wiping out some words on a blackboard.

'That's what I say in front of her, because she likes it. The truth is she has excellent common sense, and she's rarely wrong in her judgements of other people. I get too enthusiastic. I trust them too easily.'

'So she's a sort of safety catch for you.'

'If you like. I'm determined, as soon as I can get my divorce, to make her my legal wife. She practically is already.'

It was clear that the conversation was getting more difficult for him, and he was searching for words, staring at the ash on his cigar.

'How shall I put it? Nora is indeed a superior being, but she can't help being jealous. That's why in her presence, last night, I was obliged to lie to you.'

'The scene in the hotel bedroom?'

'Exactly. It didn't happen the way I told it, of course. It's true that Sophie had taken refuge in the bedroom to cry, after some cruel words spoken by Nora to her, I don't know what exactly, because we had all had a lot to drink.

'So, long story short, I went in there to comfort her.'

'And you ended up making love to her?'

'If you want to put it that way. She fell into my arms, one thing led to another, and we were very indiscreet. Very indiscreet.'

'And your wife witnessed it?'

'Well, a police officer would not have hesitated to regard it as evidence of adultery.'

He was smiling a rather satisfied smile.

'Tell me, Monsieur Carus. I imagine that you have a procession of pretty girls coming into your offices every day. And most of them would do anything to get a part in a film.'

'Very true.'

'And I'm guessing that you may sometimes take advantage of your visitor.'

'I don't hide it.'

'Even from Nora?'

'Let me explain. If now and then I take advantage, as you put it, of a pretty girl, Nora doesn't worry too much, as long as it doesn't last. It comes with the job. All men do the same thing, though they don't all have the same opportunity. Yourself, chief inspector . . .'

Maigret looked at him forbiddingly, without smiling.

'Oh, please forgive me if I shocked you. Where was I? I know that you have been questioning some of our friends, and that you will be doing so again. I prefer to be perfectly frank with you. You heard the way Nora referred to Sophie.

'I wouldn't want you, after that, to get the wrong idea about the poor girl.

'She wasn't ambitious, on the contrary, and she wasn't the kind of girl to sleep around.

'When she was very young, almost a child still, she fell for Ricain, which was inevitable, because he has a certain magnetism. Women are impressed by tortured souls, men who are ambitious, bitter and violent . . .'

'Is that how you see him?'

'What about you?'

'I haven't made up my mind yet.'

'So, she married him. She trusted him. She followed him round like a well-trained little dog, keeping her mouth shut when he didn't want her to speak, taking up as little room as possible, so as not to bother him, and accepting the precarious living she had with him.'

'Was she unhappy?'

'She was suffering from the life they led, but she didn't let him see it. And while he needed her, or rather needed her passive presence, there were moments when he was irritable towards her, calling her a dead weight, an obstacle to his career, and accusing her of being as stupid as a dumb animal.'

'She told you that?'

'I'd already guessed it from hearing some exchanges between them in front of me.'

'And she began to confide in you?'

'If you like. Not that I wanted her to, let me assure you. She felt quite lost in a world that was too hard-bitten for her, and she didn't have anyone to cling to.'

'When did you become lovers?'

'Another word I don't like. It was really mostly pity and affection I felt for her. My intention was to help her.'

'To have a career in films?'

'This will surprise you, but I did have that idea, and she was the one who was less keen. She wasn't a raving beauty like Nora, one of those women who make heads turn in the street.

'But I have a good idea of what the public likes. If I didn't, I wouldn't be in this job. With her girl-next-door looks and her delicate, slim little body, Sophie was almost exactly the image of a young girl that most people have in mind. Parents would have been able to identify her with their daughter, young men with their cousin, or girlfriend. Do you see what I'm getting at?'

'So you were planning to launch her career?'

'Let's say I was thinking about it.'

'And you spoke to her about it?'

'Not in so many words. I sounded her out discreetly.'

'And where did these conversations happen?'

'That's an awkward question, but I'm obliged to reply, I suppose?'

'Particularly since I'd find out sooner or later.'

'All right. Well, I've rented a small furnished apartment, quite pretty and comfortable, in Rue François-Ier. To be more precise, it's in the big building on the corner of Avenue Georges-V. Just three hundred metres or so from here.'

'Wait a moment. This apartment was intended exclusively for your meetings with Sophie, or was it used for other rendezvous?'

'In theory, it was for Sophie. It was difficult to find anywhere private here, and I couldn't go to her place.'

'Did you ever go there when her husband was absent?'

'Once or twice.'

'Recently?'

'The last time was about a fortnight ago. She hadn't telephoned me as she usually did, and I didn't find her in Rue François-Ier. I called her at home and she said she wasn't feeling good.'

'She was ill?'

'Discouraged. Francis was getting increasingly depressed. Sometimes he even got violent. She was at the end of her tether. She wanted to run away anywhere, work as a shop assistant in the first store that would hire her.'

'But you advised her not to do anything of the kind?'

'I gave her the address of one of my lawyers, so that she could consult him about a possible divorce. That would have been the best thing for both of them.'

'And had she decided on that?'

'She was hesitating. She felt sorry for Francis. She thought it was her duty to stay with him until he had some success.'

'Did she talk to him about it?'

'Certainly not.'

'How can you be so sure?'

'Because there would have been a violent reaction.'

'I'd like to ask you a question, Monsieur Carus. Think before you reply, because I won't conceal from you that it's important. Did you *know* that about a year ago, Sophie was pregnant?'

He went crimson, and nervously crushed out his cigar in the crystal ashtray.

'Yes, I did know,' he murmured, sitting down again. 'But let me tell you right away, and I'll swear this on all that's most precious to me, the child was not mine. At the relevant time, we didn't have intimate relations.

'I should add that it was on that account that she started confiding in me. I noticed that she was sad and preoccupied. I got a confession out of her. She admitted that she was expecting a child, and that Francis would be furious.'

'Why?'

'Because it would have been one more burden, one more obstacle in the way of his career. He was already quite unable to make ends meet. With a child . . . In short, she was sure he would never forgive her and she asked me for the address of some doctor or midwife willing to help.'

'And you gave her one?'

'I have to admit I broke the law.'

'It's a bit late now to deny it.'

'I was doing her a favour.'

'And Francis never knew?'

'No, he's too wrapped up in himself to be interested in what's going on round him, even if it concerns his wife.'

Carus stood up hesitantly and, no doubt to hide his embarrassment, went to fetch some bottles of cooled beer from the bar.

People called him Monsieur Gaston, with respectful familiarity, since he was a serious and dignified man, fully conscious of the responsibilities weighing on the shoulders of a concierge in a grand hotel. He had spotted Maigret before the inspector had even come through the revolving door, and had frowned, as the faces of guests likely to occasion a visit from the police flashed through his mind.

'Wait a moment, Lapointe.'

He waited in turn, as an old lady in front of him checked the time of arrival of a plane from Buenos Aires. Then he discreetly shook hands with Monsieur Gaston.

'Don't worry. Nothing bad.'

'When I see you come in, I always wonder . . .'

'If I'm not mistaken, Monsieur Carus has an apartment here on the fourth floor?'

'That's right. With Madame Carus.'

'She's registered under that name?'

'Well, it's the one we address her by.'

Monsieur Gaston hardly had to smile to make himself understood.

'Is she up there?'

A glance at the board carrying the room keys.

'I don't know why I looked. Just habit. At this time of day, she's certainly having her breakfast.'

'Monsieur Carus went away this week, I believe?'

'Wednesday and Thursday. Yes.'

'Alone?'

'His chauffeur drove him to Orly Airport at five o'clock. I think he was taking a plane to Frankfurt.'

'And when did he get back?'

'Yesterday afternoon, from London.'

'And although you are not on duty at night, would you

perhaps be able to tell me whether Madame Carus went out on Wednesday evening, and what time she came back?'

'Yes, that's simple.'

He leafed through the pages of a large black-bound ledger.

'When they come in at night, our guests usually stop for a moment to tell the night porter what time they wish to be woken, and give their order for breakfast.

'Madame Carus always does that. We don't make a note of the time, but from the position of names on the page, it's possible to know roughly when it was.

'So let me see . . . Only about ten names on Wednesday before hers. Miss Trevor, an elderly unmarried lady, goes to bed early, always in by ten . . . The Maxwells . . . At a guess, I'd say she was in by midnight, let's say between ten and midnight. At any rate, before people come out of the theatres. This evening I can ask my colleague the night porter to confirm that.'

'Thank you. Would you call to let her know I'm coming up?'

'You want to see her? Do you know her?'

'I had coffee last night with her and her husband. This is just a courtesy call.'

'Room 403, please . . . Hello? . . . Madame Carus? . . . The concierge here . . . Detective Chief Inspector Maigret is asking if he may come up . . . Yes . . . All right . . . I'll tell him.'

And to Maigret:

'She asks if you would give her about ten minutes.'

Would that be in order to complete her terrifying and sophisticated make-up, or to telephone to Rue de Bassano?

Maigret rejoined Lapointe and they both wandered about without speaking, looking at the display cases and admiring the jewels on show from the principal Paris jewellers, along with the fur coats and the lingerie.

'Not thirsty, are you?'

'No thanks.'

They had the unpleasant feeling that people were watching them, and it was a relief when the ten minutes were up, and they could take the lift.

'Fourth floor, please.'

Nora, who came to open the door to them herself, was wearing a pale green satin peignoir, matching her eyes, and her hair looked even more bleached than the night before, almost white.

The sitting room was vast, lit by two large bay windows, one of them opening on to a balcony.

'I wasn't expecting your visit. I've only just got up.'

'I hope we weren't interrupting your breakfast.'

The tray was not in here, but no doubt in the bedroom beyond.

'Was it my husband you wanted to see? He went to the office some time ago.'

'No, I'd just like to ask you a few questions while we're here. Of course, you are not under any obligation to reply. First of all – and it's an entirely routine question I'm putting to everyone who knew Sophie Ricain – don't take it as in any way threatening: Where were you on Wednesday evening?'

She did not flinch, but sat down in a white armchair and asked:

'At what time?'

'Where did you have dinner?'

'Wait a moment . . . Wednesday . . . Yesterday, we were with you . . . Thursday, I dined alone at Fouquet's, not upstairs, where I go with Carus, but at a little table on the ground floor . . . Wednesday . . . Wednesday, oh, I didn't eat dinner at all, it's quite simple.

'I should say that apart from a light breakfast, I usually only eat one proper meal a day. If I have lunch I don't dine, and if I dine, it's because I haven't had lunch. On Wednesday we lunched at the Berkeley with some friends.

'Then in the afternoon, I went to a fitting, just nearby. Then I had a drink at Jean's, Rue Marbeuf. And I must have got back here at about nine o'clock.'

'And then you came straight upstairs?'

'That's right. I read a book until one in the morning, because I can't get to sleep earlier. And before that I watched television.'

There was a TV set in a corner of the room.

'Don't ask me what the programme was called. All I know is there were a lot of young singers, men and women. Will that do? Should I call the porter on this floor? It's true it might not be the same one. But this evening, you could ask the night porter.'

'Did you order anything from him?'

'A quarter-bottle of champagne.'

'What time was that?'

'I don't know. Not long before I got ready for bed. Do

you suspect me of having gone to Rue Saint-Charles and killed poor Sophie?'

'I don't suspect anyone. I'm just doing my job, and trying not to be too indiscreet. Last night, you spoke of Sophie in a way that suggested there was no love lost between you.'

'I didn't try to hide it.'

'There was mention of one evening here, when you discovered her in your husband's arms.'

'I shouldn't have mentioned it. It was just to let you know she'd throw herself at any man. She was neither the little innocent nor the besotted wife of Francis that other people may have told you about.'

'Who do you mean?'

'Oh, I don't know. Men tend to be taken in by that kind of performance. Most of the people in our circle probably think of me as a cold, calculating and ambitious female. Admit it!'

'No one has described you in such terms to me.'

'I'm sure it's what they all think. Even someone like Bob, who must have plenty of experience. Little Sophie, by contrast, sweet and resigned, is seen as a misunderstood and lovelorn girl. Well, think what you like. I've told you the truth.'

'Was Carus her lover?'

'Who says so?'

'Well, you told me yourself you had surprised them.'

'I said she'd fallen into his arms, and was snivelling in order to get his sympathy, but I didn't claim Carus was her lover . . .'

'But the other men all were, is that it? That's what you're getting at?'

'Ask them. See if they dare to lie to you.'

'What about Ricain? Did he know?'

'You're putting me in a difficult position. It's not up to me to pass judgement on people we meet who are not necessarily our friends. Did I say that Francis knew all about it? I may have done. I don't remember. I tend to speak impulsively, on the spur of the moment.

'Carus has taken a real shine to that boy, predicting he has a fantastic future ahead of him. *I* think he's a cunning young man pretending to be an artist. Take your pick.'

Maigret was getting up, taking his pipe from his pocket.

'Well, that's all I wanted to ask you. Oh, just one more minor point. Sophie was a few months pregnant about a year ago.'

'Yes, I know.'

'She told you?'

'She was about two or three months gone, I forget which. Francis didn't want children, because of his career. So she asked me if I knew any addresses. People had told her she could go to Switzerland, but she was hesitating about taking the trip.'

'Were you able to help her?'

'I told her I didn't know anyone. I didn't want Carus and myself to get mixed up in something like that.'

'How did it end?'

'From her point of view, it must have ended all right, because she didn't mention it again and she never had a child.'

'Thank you for your time.'

'You haven't been to Carus' office?'

Maigret replied to her question with another question:

'He hasn't phoned you?'

He was sure, after this, that once she was alone, the young woman would put a call through to Rue de Bassano.

'Thank you, Gaston,' he said, as he went past the concierge.

On the pavement he took a deep breath.

'If we end up having a general confrontation, it looks as if fur will fly.'

As if to rinse out his mouth, he went into the nearest bar and drank a glass of white wine. He'd been longing for one all morning, ever since his visit to Rue Saint-Louis-en-l'Ile, and Carus' beer hadn't taken the desire away.

'Now back to headquarters, young Lapointe, I'm curious to find out what state we'll find our Francis in.'

He wasn't in the glass-panelled cage, where there was no one except an old woman accompanying a youth with a broken nose. In his office, Maigret found Janvier, who pointed to Ricain: the young man was sitting on a chair looking furious.

'I had to bring him in here, chief. He was making a terrible row in the corridor, wanting the usher to take him straight to the chief of police, threatening to call the newspapers.'

'It's my right!' Ricain burst out angrily. 'I've had enough of being treated like an imbecile or a criminal! My wife's been killed and I'm being kept under observation as if I might run away. I'm not left a moment's peace, and—'

'Do you want a lawyer?'

Francis looked him in the eye, hesitating, his expression full of hate.

'You . . . You . . .'

His rage prevented him finding the words.

'You act like you're so fatherly. You must be very pleased with yourself for being so kind, so patient, so understanding. And I fell for it too. But now I can see that all the stuff they wrote about you is rubbish.'

He was stammering, the words were tumbling out faster and faster.

'How much do you pay the journalists to make them sing your praises? What a fool I was! When I saw your name in the wallet, I thought I was saved, that at last I'd found someone who would *understand*.

'So I called you. Because without my phone call, you'd never have found me. I could have used your money to . . . When I think that I didn't even keep enough to get a bite to eat.

'And what's the result? You lock me up in some cheap hotel, with an inspector on the pavement outside.

'Then you shut me in your rat-trap and your men come and peer at me all the time through the glass. I've counted at least twelve of them who've been along to take a good look.

'And all this because my wife was killed in my absence, and the police are incapable of protecting citizens. Because, instead of looking for the real killer, they pick on the obvious suspect, the husband, who's had the misfortune of having panicked.'

Maigret drew slowly on his pipe, facing Francis, who was beside himself and on his feet now in the middle of the room, waving his arms about with clenched fists.

'Have you finished?'

He put the question in a calm voice, without impatience or irony.

'Do you still want to have a lawyer?'

'I can defend myself. You'll have to recognize at some point that you've made a mistake, and let me go—'

'You're free.'

'You mean . . .?'

His rage suddenly subsided and he stood there, arms hanging down, looking at Maigret incredulously.

'You've been free all along, you know that quite well. If I arranged a place for you to stay last night, it was because you didn't have any money, and I supposed you didn't want to go back to sleep in the apartment in Rue Saint-Charles.'

Maigret had pulled his wallet from his pocket, the same wallet that Francis had stolen from him on the platform of the bus. He took out two ten-franc notes.

'Here's something to get a bite to eat and take you back to the Grenelle neighbourhood. One of your friends will certainly lend you some money for your immediate needs. I should tell you I have sent a telegram to your wife's parents in Concarneau, and her father will be arriving in Paris this evening. I don't know whether he will contact you. I didn't speak to him myself, but I understand he would like to take his daughter's body back to Brittany.'

Ricain was not talking about leaving now. He was trying to understand.

'Of course, as her husband, you must be the one to decide.'

'What would you advise?'

'Funerals are expensive. And I don't imagine you would often have time to visit the cemetery. So if that's what the family wants . . .'

'I'll have to think about it.'

Maigret had opened the door of his cupboard, where he always kept a bottle of cognac and glasses, a precaution which had often proved useful.

He filled only one glass and passed it to the young man.

'Drink up.'

'What about you?'

'No thanks.'

Francis drank the cognac in a single gulp.

'Why are you giving me alcohol?'

'To get you back on your feet.'

'I suppose I'll be followed?'

'No, we won't even do that. Provided you let me know where I can reach you. Will you go back to Rue Saint-Charles?'

'Where else could I go?'

'One of my inspectors is there at the moment. By the way, last night your phone rang twice. He picked it up and both times nobody spoke at the other end.'

'Well, it couldn't have been me, because . . .'

'I'm not asking if it was you. Someone else called your number. Perhaps someone who hadn't seen the papers. What I'm wondering is whether this man or woman was expecting to hear your voice or your wife's.'

'I wouldn't know.'

'Has it ever happened to you, picking up the phone and only hearing someone breathing?'

'Is there some theory behind this?'

'Supposing whoever it was expected to find that you weren't there, and wanted to talk to Sophie?'

'Again? What have they been telling you, the people you've been questioning last night and again this morning? What grubby gossip are you trying to—?'

'One question, Francis.'

He gave a start, surprised to hear himself called by this name.

'What did you do last year, when you discovered that Sophie was pregnant?'

'She's never been pregnant.'

'We have a medical report. Janvier?'

'Here it is, chief. Delaplanque just brought it over.'

Maigret glanced through it.

'Look here. You'll see I'm not making things up, simply referring to the medical evidence.'

Ricain glared at him again savagely.

'My God, what is this, what's it all about? Have you decided to drive me mad? One minute you're accusing me of killing my wife, the next—'

'I've never accused you.'

'Well, as good as. You've insinuated it. Then to calm me down . . .'

He picked up the glass he had drunk the cognac from and hurled it violently to the floor.

'I ought to have wised up about all your little tricks. It'd make a good film, wouldn't it? But the Prefecture would certainly ban it. So Sophie was pregnant, a year ago? And naturally, since we don't have a child, I suppose you think we went to a backstreet abortionist? Is that it? Is this some new accusation you've found to pin on me, because the other one wouldn't stick?'

'I never claimed you knew about it. I was asking whether your wife had told you about it. In fact, she asked someone else for help.'

'Because it was somebody else's business, and not mine, her husband's?'

'She wanted to avoid trouble for you, and perhaps for you not to have it on your conscience. She thought that a child, at this point in your career, would simply be a burden.'

'So?'

'She confided in one of your friends.'

'Who, for God's sake?'

'Carus.'

'What? You want me to believe that it was to Carus that—'

'He told me about it this morning. Nora confirmed it half an hour later, but with a slight difference. According to her, Sophie wasn't alone when she told Nora about this pregnancy. You were both there.'

'She was lying, then.'

'That's possible.'

'Do you believe her?'

'For the time being, I don't believe anyone.'

'Including me?'

'Including you, Francis. All the same, you're free to go.'

And Maigret relit his pipe, sat down at his desk, and started leafing through a file.

6.

Ricain had left, his manner hesitant and awkward, like a bird suspiciously contemplating its open cage door, and Janvier had looked inquiringly at his chief. Were they really letting him out on to the streets without any surveillance?

Maigret, pretending not to understand this unspoken question, went on studying his file, then stood up at last with a sigh and went to stand at the window.

He was in a bad mood. Janvier had returned to the inspectors' office where he and Lapointe were exchanging impressions in low voices when Maigret entered the room. The two inspectors instinctively moved apart, but it was unnecessary. Maigret did not seem to see them.

He was wandering from one desk to another as if he did not know what to do with his bulky body, stopping in front of a typewriter, a telephone or an empty chair, moving a sheet of paper for no reason.

In the end, he muttered:

'Get a message to my wife that I won't be home for lunch.'

He was not calling her himself, which was a bad sign. No one dared speak, let alone ask him any questions. In the inspectors' office, everyone was on tenterhooks, he could feel it, and, with a shrug, he went back into his own office and fetched his hat.

He said nothing, neither where he was going, nor when he would be back, and left no instructions, as if suddenly he had lost interest in the whole affair.

On the wide dusty staircase, he emptied his pipe by tapping it against his heel, then crossed the courtyard, vaguely saluted the man on duty, and set off towards Place Dauphine.

Perhaps that wasn't where he really wanted to go. His mind was elsewhere, in that neighbourhood unfamiliar to him: Grenelle, Rue Saint-Charles, Avenue de La Motte-Picquet.

He saw again the dark line of the overhead Métro cutting diagonally across the sky, and thought he could hear the rumble of carriages. The enclosed, rather sickly-sweet atmosphere of the Vieux-Pressoir; Rose, wiping her hands on her apron all the time with a cheerful air, and the waxen features of the former stuntman with the ironic smile.

Maki, huge and mild-mannered, sitting in his corner, his gaze becoming vaguer and more lost as he drank . . . Gérard Dramin, with his pale ascetic face, endlessly correcting his screenplay . . . Carus, who went to such lengths to be friendly to everyone, and Nora, artificial from her fingertips to her bleached hair . . .

It was as if his steps were taking him, unconsciously, from force of habit, to the Brasserie Dauphine, and he automatically greeted the owner, sniffed the warm smells inside the restaurant, and headed for his usual corner, where he had sat thousands of times on the same banquette.

'There's andouillette on the menu today, chief inspector.'

'With mashed potatoes?'

'And what would you like as a starter?'

'Whatever you've got. And a carafe of Sancerre.'

His colleague from Special Branch was dining in the other corner with a civil servant from the Ministry of the Interior, whom Maigret knew only by sight. The other customers were almost all regulars; lawyers who would soon be crossing the square to go into court, an examining magistrate and an inspector from the Gambling Squad.

The restaurant owner too understood this was not the moment to start chatting, and Maigret ate slowly, with a concentrated air, as if it was a matter of some importance.

Half an hour later, he was turning the corner of the Palais de Justice, slowly, hands behind his back, without taking interest in anything in particular, like a lonely man taking the dog for a walk, and finally he found himself on the staircase; he pushed open the door to his office.

A note from Gastinne-Renette was waiting for him. It wasn't the definitive report. But the pistol found in the Seine was indeed the gun that had fired the shot in Rue Saint-Charles.

He shrugged once more, since he already knew this. At times, he felt overwhelmed by all these secondary questions, reports, phone calls and routine comings and goings.

Joseph, the old usher, tapped on his door and as usual came in without waiting for a reply.

'There's a gentleman—'

Maigret held out his hand, glanced at the form.

'Show him in.'

The man was wearing black, contrasting with his highly coloured cheeks and his shock of grey hair.

'Sit down, Monsieur Le Gal. My condolences.'

The man had had time to weep in the train, and it seemed likely that in order to give himself courage he had had a few strong drinks. His eyes wandered and he found it difficult to get his words out.

'What have they done with her? I didn't want to go to their address in case I met that man, because I think I'd strangle him with my bare hands.'

How many times had Maigret witnessed the same reactions on the part of families?

'In any case, Monsieur Le Gal, her body is not in Rue Saint-Charles but in the Forensic Institute.'

'Where's that?'

'Near the Pont d'Austerlitz, on the embankment. I'll have you driven over there, since it's essential that you officially identify your daughter.'

'Did she suffer?'

He was clenching his fists but without conviction. It could be sensed that his energy had evaporated, along with his anger, as the kilometres had rolled past, so that now his head was empty, and he was merely mouthing words he no longer believed.

'I hope you've arrested him.'

'There is no evidence against her husband.'

'But look, inspector, the day she told us about that man, I could see it would end badly.'

'Did she bring him to see you?'

'No, I've never met him. All I've seen is some blurred

photograph. She didn't want to introduce him to us. As soon as she met him, her family ceased to exist for her.

'All she wanted was to get married as quickly as possible. She'd even prepared the letter of consent for me to sign. Her mother didn't want me to do it. But I gave in in the end, so I think I must be a bit responsible for what happened.'

In every case, there was always, like this, something both moving and sordid.

'Was she your only child?'

'No, luckily we have a son, he's fifteen.'

In fact, Sophie had long ago disappeared from their lives.

'Will I be able to take her body back to Concarneau?'

'As far as we're concerned, the formalities are over.'

The word he had used was 'formalities'.

'Have they . . . I mean, was there a . . .?'

'A post-mortem, yes. To arrange transport I would advise you to consult a funeral director, they'll take care of everything.'

'What about him?'

'I've spoken to him about it. He has no objection to her being buried in Concarneau.'

'I hope he's not intending to come? Because in that case, I won't answer for anything. There are people back home with shorter fuses than me.'

'I know. I'll make sure he stays in Paris.'

'He did it, didn't he?'

'I assure you that I don't know that.'

'Who else would have killed her? She saw everything

through his eyes. He'd literally hypnotized her. Since she got married, she's not written to us as much as three times; she didn't even send us greetings at New Year.

'It was only through the newspapers that I found her new address. I thought they were still in the little hotel in Montmartre where they lived after the wedding. A funny sort of wedding anyway, no parents, or friends. Would you see that leading to a good future?'

Maigret listened to the end, nodding his head sympathetically, then closed the door behind his visitor, whose breath had smelled strongly of spirits.

And what about Ricain's father? He would no doubt turn up as well. Maigret was expecting him. He'd sent an inspector to Orly and another to the Hotel Raphaël to photograph the page of the register that the concierge had shown him.

'There are two journalists here, sir.'

'Tell them to talk to Janvier.'

A little later, Janvier put his head round the door.

'What shall I say to them, chief?'

'Anything you like. That the investigation is ongoing.'

'They thought they'd find Ricain here, so they brought along a photographer.'

'Let them look for him. They can go and ring the bell in Rue Saint-Charles if they want.'

He was ponderously following the course of his thoughts, or rather the different and contradictory thoughts going through his mind. Had he been right to let Ricain go free in his over-excited state?

He wouldn't get far with the twenty francs Maigret had

given him. He'd have to start going in search of money again, knocking on doors, doing the rounds of his friends.

'All the same, it's not *my* fault that . . .'

It was almost as if Maigret had a bad conscience about it, as if he was blaming himself for something. He kept going back to the very beginning of the case, to the platform of the bus.

He could see again the woman with the empty stare and the string bag that kept hitting his legs. A chicken, butter, eggs, leeks, celery. He had wondered why she had gone shopping so far from home.

A young man had been smoking a pipe that was too short and thick to be any good. His hair had been as fair as Nora's bleached coiffure.

At that moment, he had not yet set eyes on Carus' mistress who, at the Hotel Raphaël and elsewhere, passed for his wife.

He had briefly lost his footing on the bus, and someone had deftly removed his wallet from his hip pocket.

He would have liked to be able to dissect that instant in some way, because it seemed to him the most important. The stranger jumping from the moving bus in Rue du Temple and dashing in a zigzag course through the shoppers towards the narrow lanes of the Marais.

His image was very clear in Maigret's mind. He was sure that he would recognize him, because the thief had turned round.

Why had he turned round? And why, when he had discovered Maigret's identity, thanks to the wallet's contents, had he put it in a brown envelope and sent it back to its owner?

At that time, the moment of the theft, Ricain had believed he was a wanted man. He was sure that he would be accused of his wife's murder and locked up. The reason he had given for his desire not to be arrested was an odd one: claustrophobia.

It was the first time in thirty years that Maigret had heard a suspect give this explanation for going on the run. On reflection, though, he was obliged to admit that it could sometimes be the case. He himself took the Métro only when there was no alternative, because he felt unable to breathe there.

And why did he have a compulsion, when in his office, to go over to the window all the time?

He was sometimes met with disapproval, especially from the prosecutor's office, for doing in person tasks which should be handled by his inspectors, leaving headquarters to interrogate witnesses on the spot instead of having them summoned, revisiting the crime scene for no good reason, even taking over surveillance duties, rain or shine.

He was fond enough of his office, but he couldn't stay there for two hours without feeling the need to escape. During an investigation, he would have liked to be everywhere at once.

Bob Mandille must be taking a nap now, since the Vieux-Pressoir stayed open late at night. Did Rose have a siesta too? What would she have said if they had been sitting facing each other over a table in the empty restaurant?

Everyone had a different opinion of Ricain and Sophie. And some people even expressed contradictory views within the space of a few hours, Carus for instance.

Who was Sophie, really? The kind of girl who threw herself at any man? Or an ambitious woman who had thought that someone like Francis would offer her the life of a film star?

She was in the habit of meeting the film producer in a love nest in Rue François-Ier. If Carus was telling the truth, that is.

Ricain's jealousy had been mentioned, and apparently he was never far from his wife's side. On the other hand, he didn't hesitate to borrow money from her lover.

Did he know? Did he turn a blind eye?

'Someone to see me?'

As he had expected. The father. Ricain's this time, a large, sturdy man, still youthful-looking despite the grey crew-cut hair.

'I wasn't sure about coming.'

'Sit down, Monsieur Ricain.'

'Is he here?'

'No. He was here this morning, but he's left.'

The man had deeply etched features, bright eyes and a thoughtful expression.

'I'd have come before, but I was driving the Paris–Vintimille express.'

'When did you last see Francis?'

The other man repeated, in surprise:

'Francis?'

'That's what his friends all call him.'

'Well, at home he was François. Let me see. He turned up to see me just before Christmas.'

'Were you on good terms?'

'I saw him so rarely!'

'What about his wife?'

'He introduced her to me a few days before they got married.'

'How old was he when his mother died?'

'Fifteen. He was a good boy, but already a bit difficult; he didn't like to be crossed. It was a waste of time trying to stop him doing something if he was set on it. I wanted him to go into the railways. Not necessarily manual work, he could have got a good office job.'

'Why did he come to see you before Christmas?'

'To ask me for money, of course. The only reason he ever came. He didn't have any proper work. He scribbled and thought he was going to be a famous writer.'

'I did my best . . . I couldn't exactly tie him up . . . I was often away for three days on end. It wasn't much fun for him to come home to an empty house and have to make his own meals. What do *you* think, inspector?'

'I just don't know.'

The man looked surprised. That a senior official in the police force should not have a definite opinion was beyond his understanding.

'You don't think he's guilty?'

'So far, there's nothing to prove it one way or the other.'

'You think that woman was right for him? She didn't bother to wear a dress when he brought her to see me, she was in trousers with sloppy shoes, she hadn't even combed her hair. It's true you see girls like that everywhere in the street now.'

There was quite a long silence, during which Monsieur

Ricain glanced several times at Maigret. Finally, he pulled a battered wallet from his pocket and took out several hundred-franc notes.

'It's best if I don't go to see him. If he wants to see me, he knows where I live. I expect he's still short of money. He might need it to pay a good lawyer.'

A pause. A question.

'Do you have children, inspector?'

'Unfortunately not.'

'He mustn't feel he's been abandoned. Whatever he's done, if he's done something bad, he's not responsible. Tell him that's what I think. Tell him he's welcome to come to the house whenever he wants. But I won't force him. I understand.'

Touched, Maigret looked down at the banknotes which a large calloused hand with square fingernails was pushing across the desk.

'Well,' the father sighed, standing up and twisting his hat in his hands, 'if I've got this right, there's still some hope for me that he's innocent. I'm sure he is. Whatever the papers say, I can't bring myself to believe he could do something like that.'

Maigret saw him to the door and shook the hand which he hesitantly extended.

'Should I keep on hoping?'

'One should never give up hope.'

Once he was alone, he almost called Doctor Pardon. He would have liked to have a word with him, ask him a few questions. Pardon wasn't a psychiatrist, no. Nor indeed a professional psychologist.

But in his career as a local doctor, he had seen all kinds of cases, and his views had often confirmed Maigret in his opinion.

At this time of day, Pardon would be in his surgery with a queue of twenty patients in the waiting room. Their regular monthly dinner was only scheduled for next week.

It was curious: he suddenly had, for no particular reason, a painful sensation of loneliness.

He was just one element in the complex machinery of Justice. And he had available to him specialists, inspectors, a telephone, the telegraph, all the desirable help he needed. Above him was the prosecutor's office, the examining magistrate and, in the last analysis, the judges and juries in the criminal courts.

Why was it, then, that he felt responsible? It seemed to him that the fate of a human being depended on him. He did not yet know who that was: the man or woman who had taken the pistol from the drawer of the white-painted chest and had shot Sophie.

One detail had struck him from the start, and he had still not managed to explain it. It is rare that in the course of a quarrel, or at a moment of high emotion, someone would aim at the head.

The reflex, even in a case of self-defence, is to shoot at the chest, and only professional criminals aim at the belly, knowing that a wound there is usually fatal.

From a distance of about a metre, the killer had aimed at her head. To make it look like suicide?

No, because he had left the gun in the room. At least if Ricain could be believed . . .

The couple had come home at about ten. He had needed money. Unlike his usual practice, Francis had left his wife in Rue Saint-Charles while he set off in search of Carus, or some other friend who might lend him two thousand francs.

Why had he waited until that night, if the money was needed for a payment next morning?

He had gone back to the Vieux-Pressoir, to see if the producer had arrived.

At that moment, Carus was already in Frankfurt; they had checked the flights from Orly. And he had not told Bob or any other member of the little gang where he was going.

Nora, on the other hand, was in Paris. But not in her apartment in the Raphaël as she had claimed that morning, since the concierge's register contradicted that.

Why was she lying? Did Carus know she was not in the hotel? Wouldn't he have phoned her when he got to Frankfurt?

The telephone rang.

'Hello. Doctor Delaplanque for you. Shall I put him through?'

'Yes, please . . . Hello, doctor.'

'Maigret? Forgive me for troubling you, but something's been bothering me since this morning. If I didn't mention it in the report, it's because it's very vague. During the post-mortem, I found some faint marks on the dead woman's wrists, as if they'd been held tightly. Not really proper bruises.'

'I'm listening.'

'That's all. Though I'm not saying there was a struggle,

it wouldn't have surprised me, I could imagine an aggressor grabbing the victim by her wrists and pushing her. She could have fallen on to the sofa, then got up again, and the moment when she was regaining her balance would be when the gun was fired. That would explain why the bullet was taken from the wall about one metre twenty from the floor, whereas if the young woman had been standing upright . . .'

'I see. So there are some very slight bruises are there?'

'One of the marks is clearer than the others. It could be a thumbprint, but I can't be sure. That's why I can't state this officially. See if you can make anything of it.'

'The stage I'm at, I have to try and use whatever I can. Thank you, doctor.'

Janvier was standing silently in the doorway.

He had returned to the area, alone this time, with an obstinate expression, as if now it was a matter between the Grenelle neighbourhood and him. He had walked along the Seine, stopping forty metres upstream from the Pont de Bir-Hakeim, where the pistol had been thrown into the water and fished out again; then he had headed towards the large modern apartment building on Boulevard de Grenelle.

In the end he went in, and knocked on the glass of the concierge's lodge. She was a young, attractive woman and her little sitting room was brightly lit.

After showing her his badge, he asked:

'Is it you that collects the tenants' rent?'

'Yes, inspector.'

'So you must know François Ricain?'

'They live on the courtyard side and they don't often come through this way. I mean, they didn't . . . Well, they tell me he's back. But her . . . Yes, of course I knew them, and it wasn't nice to have to be after them all the time for their rent. In January, they asked me for a postponement of a month, then on the 15th of February another one. The landlord decided to evict them if by the 15th of March they didn't pay the two quarters owing.'

'And they haven't?'

'The 15th of March was the day before yesterday.'

Wednesday.

'And you weren't anxious when they didn't turn up?'

'I wasn't expecting them to be paying. In the morning, he didn't come by to pick up his post and I told myself he preferred to avoid me. They didn't get many letters, anyway. Just catalogues and magazines he had subscriptions to. In the afternoon, I went to knock at their door, and there was no answer.

'On Thursday morning, I knocked again, but since there was still no answer, I asked one of the tenants if she had heard anything. I even thought they might have done a midnight flit. It would be easy, because the street door on to Rue Saint-Charles is always open.'

'What's your opinion of Ricain?'

'I can't say I took much notice of him. Now and then, a tenant would complain because they were playing music or having friends round into the small hours, but there are other people who do that in the building, especially the young ones. He seemed to be an artist of some kind.'

'What about her?'

'What can I say? They were obviously short of money . . . Can't have been much fun for them. Are they sure she didn't kill herself?'

He was learning nothing new, and perhaps he wasn't even trying too hard to do so. He wandered about, looking at the nearby streets, the houses, the open windows, peering into the small shops.

At seven o'clock, he pushed the door of the Vieux-Pressoir and was almost disappointed not to see Fernande perched on her bar stool.

Bob Mandille, seated at a table, was reading the evening paper, while the waiter was finishing the place-settings, putting on each checked tablecloth a crystal vase containing a rose.

'Ah, look who's here! The inspector.'

Bob got up and shook hands with Maigret.

'So what have you found out? The journalists are complaining. They're saying there's a mystery about this whole affair and they're being kept at arms' length.'

'That's simply because we have nothing to tell them.'

'Is it true that you've released Francis?'

'He was never under arrest, and he's free to go. Who told you that?'

'Huguet, the photographer, who lives in the same block of flats, on the fourth floor. The one with two wives, and a third woman with a child on the way. He saw Francis in the courtyard as he was going back to his place. I was surprised he didn't come to see me. Tell me, has he got any money?'

'I gave him twenty francs to get something to eat and take the bus home.'

'Well, in that case, he won't be long. Unless he's gone over to the newspaper he works for, and by some miracle there's money for him there. It sometimes happens.'

'You didn't see Nora on Wednesday night?'

'No, she wasn't in. I don't think I've ever seen her without Carus, and he was abroad.'

'Yes, in Germany. She went out alone. So I'm wondering where she went.'

'She didn't tell you?'

'She claims she returned to the Raphaël at about nine p.m.'

'And that isn't true?'

'The concierge's register suggests it was more like eleven o'clock.'

'That's odd.'

Bob gave a thin ironic smile that traced a kind of crack in his reconstructed face.

'You think it's funny?'

'Well, you have to admit Carus was asking for it! He takes any chance he can get. It would be funny if Nora was also . . . But I don't believe that, actually.'

'Because she loves him?'

'No, because she's too smart and too calculating. She wouldn't risk losing it all, when she's so near her goal, just for an affair, even with the most attractive man in town.'

'She was perhaps not as near her goal as you think.'

'What do you mean?'

'Carus was regularly meeting Sophie in an apartment in Rue François-Ier, which he rented for that purpose.'

'And it was as serious as that?'

'It's what he says. He also says he thought she had the makings of a film star and would have become one quite soon.'

'Are you serious? Carus? But she was the kind of girl you can see any day of the week. Just walk down the Champs-Élysées and you could pick up enough of them to fill all the cinema screens in the world.'

'Nora was aware of their liaison.'

'Well, now, I'm lost. It's true, if I had to understand the love lives of all my customers, I'd have ulcers by now. So go and tell my wife all this. She'll be annoyed with you if you don't pop in and say hello to her in the kitchen. She's fond of you. Won't you have a glass of something?'

'Later.'

The kitchen was large and more modern than he had expected. As he predicted, Rose wiped her hand on her apron before shaking his.

'So you've decided to let him go?'

'Is that so surprising?'

'I don't know what to think. Everyone that comes in here has their own little theory. Some people think Francis did it out of jealousy. Others say it was a lover she wanted to break up with. And one or two think it could be a woman taking revenge on her.'

'Nora?'

'Who suggested that?'

'Carus had a serious affair going on with Sophie. Which Nora knew about. He was planning to get her into films.'

'Is that true, or are you inventing it to get me to talk?'

'It's true. Does it shock you?'

'Me? It's a long time since anything shocked me. If you were in this business . . .'

It did not occur to her that in the Police Judiciaire too they had a certain experience of human nature.

'Only, my dear inspector, if Nora did it, you'll have a job to prove it, because she's smart enough to fool the lot of you.

'Are you eating here tonight? I've got some duck à l'orange. And before that I can offer you two or three dozen baby scallops straight in from La Rochelle. My mother sends me them. Oh yes, she's over seventy-five, and she's down at the market every morning.'

Huguet, the photographer, arrived with his companion. He was a rosy-cheeked man with a naive expression and a cheerful manner, and you would have sworn he was proud to be parading about with a woman seven months pregnant.

'Have you met? . . . Detective Chief Inspector Maigret? . . . Jacques Huguet. And his lady friend . . .'

'Jocelyne,' the photographer pointed out, as if this was important, or as if he liked pronouncing the poetic name.

And with exaggerated concern, almost as if he were mocking her:

'What will you have to drink, sweetheart?'

He was fussing around her with affectionate and tender

attentions, as if to say to the others: 'See, I'm in love and not ashamed of it. We've made love. We're expecting a child . . . and we're happy. And it doesn't bother us one bit if you find us ridiculous.'

'Now what will you young folks have to drink?'

'A fruit juice for Jocelyne. A port for me.'

'And you, Monsieur Maigret?'

'A beer.'

'Francis isn't here?'

'Were you going to meet him here?'

'No, but I thought he would be wanting to see his friends again. If only to show them that he's free and that the police hadn't been able to keep hold of him. He's like that.'

'You thought we were going to hang on to him?'

'I don't know. It's difficult to predict what the police will do.'

'Do you think he killed his wife?'

'What does it matter whether it was him or someone else? She's dead, isn't she? And if Francis killed her, he must have had good reasons.'

'What kind of reasons, in your opinion?'

'Oh, I don't know. He'd had enough of her perhaps. Or she was making scenes at home? Or she was having affairs? People should be left to live their lives, shouldn't they, sweetheart?'

Some customers were just entering who were not regulars, and who hesitated before making for a table.

'For three?'

Since the newcomers were a middle-aged couple and a young girl.

'This way, please.'

And now they were being treated to Bob's big performance: the menu, the whispered recommendations, the praise for the white house wine from the Charentes, the chaudrée . . .

Sometimes he would wink at his companions, who were still standing at the bar.

It was at that moment that Ricain came in, stopping short when he saw Maigret in the company of Huguet and the pregnant woman.

'Ah, there you are!' cried the photographer. 'So what happened to you? We thought you were in a deep dark prison cell.'

Francis made an effort to smile.

'Well, as you see, I'm here. Good evening, Jocelyne. Is it for me that you've come, inspector?'

'For the moment it's for the duck à l'orange.'

'What will you have?' asked Bob, who had passed the diners' order on to the waiter.

'Is that port you're drinking?'

He hesitated.

'No, a Scotch. Unless I owe you too much already . . .'

'For today, I'll chalk it up.'

'And tomorrow?'

'That depends on the inspector.'

Maigret was rather disconcerted by the turn of the conversation, but he supposed it was the kind of banter that circulated between members of the little gang.

'Did you go to the newspaper office?' he asked Ricain.

'Yes. How did you know?'

'You needed money . . .'

'I just got an advance of a hundred francs on what they owe me.'

'And what about Carus?'

'I didn't go to see him.'

'But you were looking for him on Wednesday evening and almost all night.'

'Well, it isn't Wednesday today.'

'It so happens,' the photographer broke in, 'that I've seen Carus. I went into the studio and he was doing a screen test with some girl I didn't know. He even asked me to take some photos.'

'Of the girl?'

Maigret wondered whether he had taken some of Sophie too.

'He'll be dining here. At least, that was what he said at three o'clock this afternoon, but you never know with him . . . Or with Nora . . . Well, actually I came across Nora too.'

'Today?'

'No, two or three days ago. It was somewhere unexpected. A little nightclub in Saint-Germain-des-Prés, where you usually only meet very young kids.'

'And when was this?' Maigret asked, paying attention suddenly.

'Let me see. It's Saturday today . . . Friday? . . . No . . . And Thursday, I went to an opening night at the ballet . . . Must have been Wednesday. I was looking to take some photos to illustrate an article on the under-twenties, and someone had mentioned this club to me.'

'What time was this?'

'About ten in the evening. Yes, I must have got there at about ten. Jocelyne was with me. What do you think, sweetheart? Ten, wasn't it? Rather a scruffy little place, but picturesque. All the boys had long hair down to their collars.'

'Did she see you?'

'No, I don't think so. She was in a corner with some man who was certainly not an under-twenty. I think he must have been the proprietor, and they looked as if they were having a serious discussion . . .'

'Did she stay long?'

'Well, I went into the two or three rooms where they were dancing. If you can call it dancing. They did what they could, crammed up against each other.

'I glimpsed her once or twice through the heads and shoulders bobbing about. She was still talking to the guy and he had taken out a pencil to write figures on a piece of paper.

'Funny, when I come to think of it. Even in everyday life, she doesn't look very real. But in that weird world, it would have been worth taking a photo.'

'But you didn't?'

'I'm not stupid. I wouldn't want to create any bother with Papa Carus. I depend on him for a good half of my daily bread.'

The others heard Maigret order:

'Another beer, Bob.'

His voice and his attitude were not quite the same.

'Can you keep me the corner table that I had last night?'

'Aren't you going to eat with us?' the photographer asked in surprise.

'Another time.'

He needed to be alone, to think. By chance, the ideas he had started to string together had just been disturbed, and now nothing made sense.

Francis was glancing at him furtively, looking anxious. Bob too was aware that there had been some change in his manner.

'You seem surprised that Nora would have gone to a place like that.'

But the inspector, turning to Huguet, asked:

'What's the name of the club?'

'You want to go and study the beatniks too? Let me think . . . the name isn't very original. It must date from the time it was just a rundown café for dropouts. Ah yes, the Ace of Spades. That's it. On the left as you go up the hill.'

Maigret drained his glass.

'Keep my table, will you,' he repeated.

A few minutes later, a taxi was taking him to Place de la Contrescarpe.

In the remains of the daylight, the club was lacklustre. There were just three long-haired male customers, and a girl in a man's waistcoat and trousers who was smoking a small cigar. A man wearing a roll-neck sweater came out of the back room and stood behind the counter, looking suspicious.

'What'll you have?'

'A beer,' Maigret said automatically.

'Anything else?'

'No.'

'No questions?'

'What do you mean?'

'I wasn't born yesterday. I know that if Detective Chief Inspector Maigret walks in here, it won't be because he's thirsty. So I'm waiting to see what it's all about.'

The man, who was evidently ready to chat, poured himself a small glass.

'Someone came in to see you on Wednesday night.'

'Well, about a hundred someones, if you'll permit me to correct you.'

'I'm talking about a woman to whom you were talking for a long time.'

'About half the people here were women, and I was talking, as you say, with plenty of them.'

'Nora.'

'Ah, now we're getting to it. So?'

'What was she doing here?'

'What she comes to do about once a month.'

'And that is?'

'To check the accounts.'

'Because . . .'

Maigret, with a jolt, had guessed the truth before the man told him.

'Because she owns this place, yes, inspector. She doesn't go round shouting it from the rooftops. I'm not sure that Papa Carus knows about it. But everyone's got a right to put their money where they like, haven't they?

'Mind, I haven't told you a thing. You can spin me some

yarn and I won't say yes or no. Even if you were to ask me whether she owns other nightclubs like this.'

Maigret looked at him inquiringly, and the man blinked to indicate yes.

'Some people can sense the way the wind's blowing,' he ended, in a jocular tone. 'It's not always the ones who think they know best that make the smartest investments. If I had three places like this for just one year, I'd be off, I'd retire to the South of France.

'So with ten of them, and that includes some in Pigalle and one on the Champs-Élysées . . .'

7.

When Maigret walked back into the Vieux-Pressoir, three tables had been put end to end and the group had started eating together. Carus, seeing him, stood up and came towards him, checked napkin in hand.

'I hope you will give us the pleasure of joining us?'

'Don't be offended if I prefer to eat in my corner.'

'Are you afraid to sit down at table with someone whom you might be obliged to arrest sooner or later?'

He was looking straight into Maigret's eyes.

'Because there's every chance that whoever killed poor Sophie might be in here tonight, isn't there? Well . . . As you wish . . . But let us at least persuade you to come and take an Armagnac with us afterwards.'

Bob had shown him to his table in the corner near the revolving door, and he had ordered the scallops and the duck à l'orange that Rose had recommended.

He could see them sideways on now, sitting in two rows. It was clear at a glance that Carus was the important person at the table. His behaviour, his attitude, his gestures, his voice and his expression were all those of a man who is aware of his value and pre-eminence.

Ricain had taken a seat opposite him with apparent reluctance, and joined in the conversation only grudgingly. Dramin was accompanied by a young woman

Maigret hadn't seen before: soberly dressed and wearing hardly any make-up, she made little impression, and Bob later told him she was a film editor.

Maki was eating a great deal, drinking hard and looking round at his companions, replying only with grunts to questions.

Huguet, the photographer, was the one who provided most of the rejoinders to the producer. He appeared to be in high spirits, and kept eyeing the rounded belly of the placid Jocelyne with the look of a satisfied owner.

It wasn't possible at this distance to follow the conversation. But from stray words, exclamations or facial expressions, Maigret could more or less work out its gist.

'We'll soon see whose turn's next,' the photographer seemed to be saying, facetiously. And his gaze at that moment alighted on the inspector.

'He's watching us. Scrutinizing us. Now that he's squeezed all he can out of Francis, he'll attack someone else. If you pull a face like that, Dramin, it could be you.'

Lone diners, watching them from a distance, envied their good spirits. Carus had ordered champagne, and two bottles were chilling in ice-buckets. Bob in person came now and then to the table to refill the glasses.

Ricain was drinking a lot. He was the one who refilled his glass most often, and did not smile at any of the photographer's jokes, which were not all in the best of taste.

'Try to look natural, Francis. Don't forget that the eye of God is watching you.'

This was aimed at Maigret. Were they more amusing when they met on other evenings?

Carus was doing his best to help Huguet lighten the atmosphere. Nora simply stared at each of them in turn with her cold gaze.

In fact, their dinner was a lugubrious affair; nobody was behaving naturally, in part perhaps because they all sensed Maigret's presence.

'I bet one day you'll make a film about this, which our good friend Carus will produce. That's the way all dramas end up.'

'Can't you just shut up?'

'Oh sorry, I didn't realize you . . .'

It was worse when silence fell around the table. In reality, they were not united by friendship. They had not chosen each other. Everyone had selfish reasons to be there. They all depended on Carus, didn't they? Nora above all, who had managed to extract from him enough money to buy those nightclubs. She had no certainty that he would marry her one day, and preferred to take her own precautions.

Did he suspect as much? Did he believe he was loved for himself?

Probably not. Carus was a realist. He needed a companion, and for now she would do quite well. He was probably pleased that she looked striking enough to attract attention wherever they went.

'There goes Carus with his girlfriend Nora. An odd couple.'

Why not? All the same, he had been Sophie's lover, and was planning to make her a star.

But that presupposed getting rid of Nora. There had

been others before her . . . As there would be others after her.

Dramin carted round with him unfinished screenplays to which Carus could give a green light. On condition he believed in Dramin's talent.

Francis was in the same position, with the difference that he behaved in a less humble and patient manner, deliberately adopting an aggressive stance, especially when he had had a few drinks.

As for Maki, he seemed to be chewing over his private thoughts alone. His sculptures were not yet finding a market. While waiting for dealers to show some interest, he was decorating film sets, good or bad, for Carus or anyone else who needed them, and was glad when he didn't have to pay for his own dinner, eating double quantities and ordering the most expensive dishes.

And then there was the photographer . . . Maigret found it harder to assess his physiognomy. At first sight, he did not count for very much. In almost every group of people who meet regularly there's someone rather naive with big bright eyes, who likes to play the clown. His apparent candour allowed him to put his foot in it, letting slip some unpleasant truth that wouldn't have been acceptable from anyone else.

Even his profession made him seem unimportant. They laughed at him and his wives who were always pregnant.

Rose, wiping her hands, came to see that everyone was satisfied, and accepted a glass of champagne without sitting down.

Bob would stroll over to Maigret from time to time.

'They're doing the best they can,' he whispered with a conspiratorial air.

Sophie was missing. They all felt it. How did Sophie behave in these situations?

She might well have looked sulky, or shy, but she would have known all the time that she was the one in whom Carus, Mr Producer, the rich man of the gang, was interested. She would have met him that very afternoon in the little bachelor pad in Rue François-Ier.

'You'll have to be patient, little girl. I'll take care of you.'

'What about Nora?'

'That won't last much longer . . . I'm working on it . . . I'm ready to pay the price.'

'And Francis?'

'At first, he'll be annoyed that you're more successful than him and making more money. But he'll get used to it. I'll give him a film to direct. Then one day, when the time is right, you can ask him for a divorce.'

Was that what had happened? Carus, after all, needed the others too. It was by launching the careers of promising young people that he made most money. Being surrounded like this by a sort of court at the Vieux-Pressoir gave him a greater sense of his own importance than dining with promoters richer and more influential than himself.

A wink from Bob, who now brought two more bottles to the big table. Ricain, exasperated by the jokes the photographer was cracking, was replying in monosyllables. You could predict the moment when he would have had enough, and would get up to walk out. As yet, he did not dare to do so, biding his time impatiently.

It was true that one of these people had probably killed Sophie, and Maigret, feeling his head swim with the heat, looked at each of their faces.

Carus had been in Frankfurt on Wednesday night. That had been confirmed from Orly Airport. And Nora, between about ten and eleven, had been checking accounts in the frantic atmosphere of the Ace of Spades.

Maki? But why would Maki have killed her? He had slept with Sophie casually, because she expected it of him – as she expected it, apparently, from all their friends. It was a way of reassuring herself, proving she was attractive and not just another star-struck teenager.

Huguet? He already had three women. It was an obsession, it seemed, just as it was to get them pregnant. One wondered how he would manage to feed all these households.

Then there was Francis.

Maigret went over Ricain's timetable again.

They'd returned to Rue Saint-Charles at ten. He needed money pressingly. He had hoped to find Carus at the Vieux-Pressoir, but Carus wasn't there. Bob had protested at the size of the sum.

He'd left Sophie at home.

Why, when he usually dragged his wife around with him?

'No!' the photographer shouted. 'Not here, Jocelyne. Don't go to sleep!' and he explained to everyone that since she was pregnant she kept falling asleep at any time, in any place.

'Some women get a craving for pickles, or pigs' trotters,

or mock turtle soup. She just sleeps, and not only does she sleep, she snores.'

Maigret stopped listening, and went back to trying to reconstruct Ricain's comings and goings until the moment the young man had stolen his wallet in Rue du Temple, on the platform of the bus.

Ricain who had not kept a centime of the money. Who had telephoned him to tell him that . . .

He packed his pipe and lit it. He too seemed to be dozing off in his corner, over his cup of coffee.

'Won't you come and take a nightcap with us, inspector?'

Carus again. Maigret decided to accept, to sit down for a moment with them.

'So,' Huguet joked. 'Who are you going to arrest? It's frightening enough to sense you over there, not missing any of our expressions. There are moments when you almost make me feel guilty myself.'

Ricain looked so unwell that no one was surprised when he left the table suddenly and headed for the toilet.

'People ought to be issued with drinking licences,' mused Maki, 'same way we have driving licences.'

The sculptor must have acquired one of these licences himself, since he had drunk glass after glass and the only effect was to make his eyes glitter and his face turn brick red.

'Always the same with him.'

'Your health, Monsieur Maigret!' Carus was saying, holding out his glass. 'I was going to say, here's to the success of your investigation, since we all want you to find out the truth as soon as possible.'

'Except for one person,' the photographer corrected him.

'Except for one, perhaps . . . Unless it isn't any of us.'

When Francis came back to the table, his eyes were red-rimmed, his face haggard. Bob, without being asked, brought him a glass of water.

'Is that better?'

'I can't take my drink any more.'

He was avoiding Maigret's eye.

'I think I'll be off to bed.'

'You won't wait for us?'

'You're forgetting I've hardly slept for three days.'

He seemed younger in his physical distress. He looked for all the world like a lanky teenager feeling sick after his first cigar, and ashamed of it.

'Goodnight.'

They watched Carus stand up and follow Ricain to the door, speaking to him in a low voice. Then the producer sat down at the table which Maigret had occupied, pushed away the coffee-cup, and filled out a cheque, while Francis waited, looking elsewhere.

'I couldn't let him down. If I'd been in Paris on Wednesday, perhaps none of this would have happened. I'd have dined here. He could have asked me for the money for the rent, then he wouldn't have had to leave Sophie on her own.'

Maigret gave a start, repeated the same sentence to himself mentally, and looked around them all again.

'Would you excuse me? I'll be leaving now.'

He needed to be outside, since he was beginning to feel stifled. Perhaps he too had had too much to drink? At any rate he did not finish the enormous glass of Armagnac.

Without any particular destination, hands in pockets, he walked along the pavements where some shop windows were still lit up. The people in the street were mainly couples who stopped to look at displays of washing machines and television sets. Young couples, dreaming and calculating.

'A hundred francs a month, Louis.'

'On top of over two hundred and fifty for the car.'

Francis and Sophie must have walked round here like this, arm in arm.

Did they dream of washing machines and television sets?

As for a car, they had one, a dilapidated old Triumph that Ricain had abandoned somewhere that famous Wednesday night. Had he gone back to pick it up?

With the cheque he had just received, he would be able to pay the rent. Did he plan on living alone in the apartment where his wife had been murdered?

Maigret crossed the boulevard. An old man was sleeping on a bench. The large modern apartment block reared up in front of him, about half its windows showing lights.

The other tenants must be out at the cinema or with friends, or perhaps lingering, like the group in the Vieux-Pressoir, at a restaurant table.

The air was still mild, but the large clouds piling up would soon obscure the full moon.

Maigret turned the corner of Rue Saint-Charles, and went inside the courtyard. A small window with frosted glass was lit near Ricain's door: that must be the window of the bathroom with the half-size bath.

Other doors, other lighted windows, both in the small ground-floor apartments and in the central building.

The courtyard was empty and silent, dustbins in their place, and a cat slinking furtively along the wall.

Now and then, a window would close and a light go out. The early-to-bed people. Then, on the fourth floor, a light went on. It was rather like the stars erratically twinkling or disappearing in the night sky.

He thought he recognized, on the fourth floor, behind a blind, the bulky silhouette of Jocelyne, and the photographer's shock of hair.

Then his gaze moved down to the ground floor.

'At about ten o'clock . . .'

He knew by heart the timetable of that night. The Huguets had dined at the Vieux-Pressoir. And since they had been alone, they had not stayed long. What time had they arrived home?

Ricain and Sophie must have opened their door and put the lights on at about ten. And then almost immediately, Francis had gone out.

Maigret could still see up above him silhouettes coming and going. Then there was only one, that of the photographer, who opened the window and looked up at the sky. Just as he was turning away, his gaze fell on the courtyard. He must have been able to see the Ricains' bathroom light and, standing in the deserted space, Maigret's silhouette, illuminated by the moon.

Maigret emptied his pipe by tapping it against his heel, and went inside the main building. Coming in from this direction, he did not need to go past the concierge's lodge. He got into the lift, pressed the button for the fourth floor, then took a moment to find his way through the corridors.

When he knocked at the door, it was as if Huguet was waiting for him to call, since he opened it at once.

'Ah, it's you!' he said with an odd smile. 'My wife's just going to bed. Do you want to come in, or would you prefer me to come outside with you?'

'It might be better if we went downstairs.'

'One moment. I'll just tell her, and fetch my cigarettes.'

Through the door, it was possible to see an untidy sitting room, and the dress Jocelyne had been wearing that evening thrown across a chair.

'No, no. I promise I'll be back up in no time.'

Then he spoke in a lower voice. She was whispering. The bedroom door was open.

'Are you sure?'

'Don't worry. Back in a few minutes.'

He never wore a hat. He did not put on a coat.

'Come along.'

The lift was still there. They used it to go down.

'Which way? The boulevard or the courtyard?'

'The courtyard.'

They reached it, and walked side by side in the darkness. When Huguet looked up, he saw his wife peering through the window, and made a sign to her to get back inside.

There was still a light on in the Ricains' bathroom. Was the young man's stomach lurching again?

'You guessed?' the photographer asked in the end, after giving a cough.

'I'm just wondering.'

'This isn't a very pleasant situation, you know. Ever since, I've tried to play the clown. Just now at the table, I spent the worst evening of my life.'

'That was obvious.'

'Have you got a match?'

Maigret passed him the box and slowly started to pack one of the two pipes he had in his pockets.

8.

'Did Ricain and his wife have dinner at the Vieux-Pressoir on Wednesday night?'

'No. Tell you the truth, they only ate there if by chance they were in funds, or if someone else was paying. They called in at about eight thirty. It was only Francis that came inside. Often, in the evening, he'd just push the door open a bit. If Carus was there, he'd come right in, followed by Sophie, and go and sit at his table.'

'And on Wednesday, did he talk to anyone?'

'When I saw him, he was just exchanging a word or two with Bob. He asked him:

' "Is Carus here?"

'And when the answer was no, he left.'

'He didn't try to borrow any money?'

'Not then.'

'If he was counting on Carus to invite him to dinner, that would mean they hadn't yet eaten?'

'They must have picked up a snack in the self-service café on Avenue de La Motte-Picquet. They often went there.'

'And did you and your wife stay long at the table?'

'We left the Vieux-Pressoir at about nine. We took the air for about a quarter of an hour. Then we went back home and Jocelyne got undressed right away. Since she's been pregnant, she's always going to sleep.'

'Yes, I heard . . .'

The photographer looked inquiringly at him.

'You talked about her during dinner. Apparently she snores.'

'My other two wives did too. I think all women must snore when they're a few months pregnant. I was saying that to tease her.'

They were talking in low voices, in the silence which was disturbed only by the sound of traffic on Boulevard de Grenelle, on the other side of the building. Rue Saint-Charles, beyond the open gate, was deserted apart from the odd passer-by they could glimpse from a distance, sometimes a woman clicking along in high heels.

'What did *you* do?'

'I saw her to bed, then I went to kiss my kids goodnight.'

It was true that his two previous wives lived in the same block, one with two children, the other with just one.

'And you do that every night?'

'Almost every night. Unless I get back too late.'

'And you're welcome there, are you?'

'Why not? My ex-wives aren't mad at me. They know me. They know I can't be other than the way I am.'

'And the way you are means that, sooner or later, you'd leave Jocelyne for someone else?'

'If the opportunity came along. You see, it's not important to me. But I adore kids. The greatest man in history, as far as I'm concerned, was Abraham.'

It was hard not to smile, since, this time, he seemed to be speaking sincerely. There was a certain underlying innocence in him, despite his questionable jokes.

'I stayed on a bit with Nicole. She's the second one. We sometimes get together for old times' sake.'

'And does Jocelyne know about that?'

'She's not bothered. If I wasn't like that, she wouldn't be with me.'

'So you made love?'

'No. It crossed my mind, but the kid started talking in his sleep, so I tiptoed out.'

'And this was what time?'

'I didn't look at my watch. I went back home. I had to change the film in one of my cameras, because I had an early-morning job on, so I automatically did that. Then I opened the window.

'I do that every night, first wide open to get rid of the cigarette smoke, then halfway because, winter or summer, I can't sleep with it closed.'

'And then?'

'I was smoking a last cigarette. There was a full moon, like tonight. I saw a couple crossing the courtyard and I recognized Francis and his wife. They weren't arm in arm as they usually were, and they were having some kind of heated conversation.'

'You couldn't hear what they said?'

'Just one sentence from Sophie, in a raised voice, that made me think she was angry.'

'Was she often angry?'

'No. She said: "Don't play the innocent – you knew perfectly well." '

'And did he reply?'

'No, he grabbed her by the elbow and dragged her towards the door.'

'And you still don't remember what time that was.'

'Yes I do, because I heard the church clock strike ten. The bathroom light went on. And I lit another cigarette.'

'Because you were intrigued?'

'No, I just wasn't ready to go to bed. I poured myself a glass of calvados.'

'You were in your living room?'

'Yes. The bedroom door was open and I'd put out the lights so as not to disturb Jocelyne.'

'And how much time went past?'

'Well, enough time to finish both the cigarette I'd started when I was over at my wife's, and then another one that I lit up when I was at the window. A bit more than five minutes. But less than ten anyway.'

'And you heard nothing?'

'No. I saw Francis come out again and walk fast towards the gates. He always parked his car in Rue Saint-Charles. After a few moments, the engine started and then the car drove off.'

'And when did you go down?'

'Quarter of an hour later.'

'Why?'

'I just told you, I wasn't ready to go to sleep. I wanted to chat.'

'Just a chat?'

'Maybe a bit more.'

'Had you had any relationship with Sophie before?'

'You mean had I slept with her? Just the once. It was this time when Francis was drunk, and since there wasn't any drink left in the house, he went out to get a bottle from whichever café was still open.'

'And she was willing?'

'She seemed to think it quite natural.'

'And after that?'

'After that, nothing. Ricain came back empty-handed, because they'd refused to sell him any alcohol. We put him to bed and that was that. The next few days, nothing else happened.'

'Let's get back to Wednesday night. You went downstairs?'

'I went to their door and knocked. And, not to frighten Sophie, I whispered:

' "It's only Jacques." '

'And there was no reply?'

'No, no sound from inside at all.'

'Did that seem odd to you?'

'I told myself she must have quarrelled with Francis and didn't want to see anyone. I imagined she'd be in bed, in tears or furious.'

'Did you insist?'

'I knocked two or three times, then I went back upstairs.'

'Did you look out of the window?'

'I'd got into pyjamas, and I glanced into the courtyard. It was empty. There was still a light on in the Ricains' bathroom. I went to bed and off to sleep.'

'Go on.'

'I got up at eight, and made coffee, while Jocelyne was

still sleeping. I opened the window wide and saw that the light was still on in Francis' bathroom.'

'Didn't *that* seem odd to you?'

'Not really. These things happen. I went to the studios, worked until one, then I grabbed a quick bite to eat with a friend. I had a meeting planned at the Ritz with an American actor who kept me waiting an hour, so I hardly had any time for his photo session. One way and another, it was four o'clock before I got home.'

'Your wife hadn't gone out?'

'To do the shopping, yes. After lunch she went to lie down, so she was asleep.'

He seemed to realize that this constant sleep leitmotif was amusing.

'And the light was . . .?'

'Still on, that's right.'

'Did you go and knock on the door?'

'No, I telephoned. Nobody answered. Ricain must have got back, fallen asleep, and then they must both have gone out and forgotten to put out the light.'

'Did that happen often?'

'Well, it happens to everyone, doesn't it? Then, let me see, Jocelyne and I went out to a cinema on the Champs-Élysées . . .'

Maigret almost muttered:

'And she went off to sleep?'

The cat came and rubbed itself against his trouser leg and looked up at him as if hoping to be stroked. But when Maigret bent down, it bounded away, stopping a couple of metres from them with a meow.

'Whose cat is that?'

'Don't know. Everyone's. People throw it scraps from their windows. It lives out here.'

'What time did you get back on Thursday night?'

'About half past ten. After the cinema, we went to have a drink in a café and I bumped into a pal.'

'And the light?'

'Yes, of course. But that wouldn't be surprising, because the Ricains might have got home. I did telephone. And I admit that, when there was no answer, I was a bit worried.'

'Just a bit?'

'Well, I wasn't going to suspect what had really happened, was I? If you thought a murder had been committed every time someone forgets to turn off a light . . .'

'So?'

'Wait. Look, just now, it's still on. But I don't think he can be up working.'

'What about next morning?'

'Well, naturally, I phoned again, and twice more during the day, until I read in the evening paper that Sophie was dead. I was out at the studios in Joinville, doing the stills for a film.'

'Did anyone reply?'

'Yes, a voice I didn't recognize. I thought it best not to say anything, so I hung up.'

'And you didn't try to get in touch with Ricain?'

Huguet said nothing. Then he shrugged and put on his comedy face again.

'Well, I'm not a detective at Quai des Orfèvres, am I?'

Maigret, who was gazing automatically at the light filtering through the frosted glass of the window, suddenly moved fast to the door of the Ricains' apartment. The photographer followed him, realization dawning.

'While we were just chatting here . . .'

If Francis wasn't working, if he wasn't asleep, and if the light had stayed on this evening . . .

The inspector banged hard on the door.

'Open up! It's Maigret!'

He made such a noise that a neighbour appeared at another door, in pyjamas, and stared at the two men in astonishment.

'What's this all about? Can't people have a bit of—'

'Go to the concierge and ask her if she's got a pass key.'

'No, she doesn't.'

'How do you know?'

'Because I asked her one night, when I'd forgotten my keys, we had to get a locksmith.'

Huguet, for someone who played the fool, had not lost his presence of mind. He wrapped a handkerchief around his fist and punched the frosted-glass window, which splintered into pieces.

'Quick!' he called breathlessly, having peered inside.

Maigret looked inside in turn. Ricain, fully dressed, was sitting in the bath, which was too small to lie down in. Water was running from the tap. The bath was overflowing and the water was pink.

'Have you got a wrench or a jack or something else heavy?'

'In my car. Hang on.'

The neighbour went back inside, and re-emerged in a dressing gown, followed by his wife asking questions. He disappeared through the gate and they heard the sound of a car boot opening. As the wife looked outside in turn, Maigret shouted to her: 'Call a doctor! Whoever's nearest.'

'What's going on? Isn't it enough that . . .?'

She went off muttering to herself, while the husband returned with a tyre iron. He was taller, broader and heavier than the inspector.

'Let me go ahead. As long as I don't have to worry about the damage . . .'

The wood resisted at first, then cracked. A couple more blows at the bottom, then the top, and the door gave way suddenly, almost pitching the man inside.

The rest happened in confusion. Other neighbours had heard the noise, and soon there were several people crowding into the entry hall. Maigret had dragged Francis out of the bath and on to the sofa-bed in the sitting room. He remembered the drawer in the chest and its motley collection of objects.

He found some string. A big blue pencil helped him devise a tourniquet. He had scarcely finished when a young doctor pushed him aside. He lived in the apartment block and had hastily slipped on a pair of trousers.

'How long ago . . .?'

'We've only just found him.'

'Phone for an ambulance.'

'Will he . . .?'

'Oh, for God's sake, don't ask questions!'

Five minutes later, an ambulance was pulling up in the courtyard. Maigret got in the front alongside the driver. In the hospital, he had to stay in the corridor while the duty doctor started a blood transfusion.

He was surprised to see Huguet turn up.

'Is he going to pull through?'

'They don't know.'

'Do you think he really meant to kill himself?'

One sensed that Huguet doubted it. As did Maigret. Cornered, Francis had needed some dramatic gesture.

'Why do you think he did it?'

The inspector misunderstood the sense of the question.

'Because he thought he was too intelligent.'

Of course, the photographer had no idea what this meant and looked at him in puzzlement.

Maigret was not thinking about Sophie's death just then. He was thinking about an event much less serious but perhaps more significant, and more important for Ricain's future: the theft of his wallet.

9.

He had slept until ten o'clock, but had not been able to eat his breakfast in front of an open window as he had promised himself, since a fine, cold rain had begun to fall.

Before going into the bathroom, where there was no window, frosted or otherwise, looking on to the courtyard, he telephoned the hospital, and had considerable trouble getting through to the duty doctor.

'Ricain, you say? . . . What's it about? . . . An emergency? . . . We had eight emergency admissions last night and if I had to remember all their names . . . OK . . . A transfusion . . . A suicide attempt . . . Ah, yes. Well, if he'd severed the artery, he wouldn't be in here at all, or we'd have had to put him in the cold store in the basement . . . Yes, he's all right . . . No, he hasn't said a word . . . No. Not a single word . . . There's a cop sitting outside his room . . . I suppose you know what it's all about . . .?'

By eleven, Maigret was in his office. His feet were hurting again, since he had decided to put on his new shoes, which he still needed to wear in.

Sitting opposite Lapointe and Janvier, he automatically lined up his pipes in order of size, chose the longest one, and packed it carefully.

'As I was saying last night to the photographer . . .'

The two inspectors glanced at each other, wondering which photographer he meant.

'As I was saying then, he's too intelligent. That can sometimes be as dangerous as being too stupid. An intelligence that isn't anchored to any strength of character. Oh, never mind. I know what I mean to say, even if I can't find quite the right words.

'And it's not my problem now. The doctors and psychiatrists will take care of it.

'I'm almost sure he was an idealist, an idealist who was unable to live up to his own ideal. Do you see what I'm getting at?'

Not very well, perhaps. Maigret had rarely been at the same time so talkative and so unclear.

'He must have wanted to be someone extraordinary in every way. To succeed very quickly, since he was bursting with impatience, yet he also wanted to remain pure.'

He felt discouraged, his sentences lagged far behind his thoughts.

'For the best and for the worst. He must have hated Carus, because he needed him so much. All the same, he accepted the dinners the producer offered him and didn't hesitate to tap him for money.

'He was ashamed of that. Angry with himself.

'He wasn't so naive as not to see that Sophie wasn't the woman he wanted her to be. But he needed her too. And he gained some advantage in the end, from her relationship with Carus.

'But he refused to admit that. He absolutely couldn't admit it.

'And that's why he shot his wife. Already when they came into the courtyard, they were quarrelling. It doesn't matter what about. She must have been exasperated at seeing him playing this questionable role, and she probably spat out the truth to his face.

'It wouldn't surprise me if she had called him a pimp. Perhaps the drawer was half-open. At any rate, he couldn't bear to hear a truth like that spoken out loud.

'So he fired the gun. Then he stood there, terrified by what he had done and the consequences.

'From that moment, I'm sure, he decided he wasn't going to pay the price for this, and his brain started working, building up, as he wandered the streets, a complicated plan.

'So complicated, in fact, that it almost succeeded.

'He goes back to the Vieux-Pressoir. Asks if Carus is there. He needs two thousand francs immediately, and he knows Bob can't possibly lend him that kind of money.

'He throws the gun into the Seine to remove the fingerprints.

'He turns up several times at Club Zéro. "Oh, hasn't Carus arrived yet?" He drinks, walks endlessly, adding finishing touches to his plan.

'It's true he doesn't have enough money to escape abroad, but even if he did, that would be no use, he'd be extradited sooner or later. What he has to do is go back to Rue Saint-Charles, pretend to discover the body, and tell the police.

'And that's when he thinks of me.

'He decides to devise a special scenario for me,

something that wouldn't occur to most normal people. The details add up. His wanderings about all night will help him.

'He lies in wait for me, from early morning, outside where I live. If I don't take the bus, he'll have some other plan up his sleeve.

'He steals my wallet. He then telephones me, and sets in motion a whole rigmarole designed to remove suspicion from him.

'And he goes too far, in fact. He gives me an entirely fictitious menu of what Sophie is supposed to have eaten at the Vieux-Pressoir. He's unbalanced, he lacks simple common sense. He can invent an extravagant story and make it sound quite plausible, but he doesn't think about the simplest, most everyday details.'

'Do you think he'll go on trial, chief?' Lapointe asked.

'Depends on the psychiatrists.'

'What would you decide?'

'Trial by jury.'

And as his two colleagues were surprised at such a categorical reply, very unlike what they knew of their chief, Maigret followed it up with:

'It would make him too unhappy to be considered of unsound mind, or even only partly responsible. When he's standing in the dock, on the other hand, he'll make sure to act out the part of an exceptional being, a kind of hero.'

He shrugged his shoulders, smiled sadly and went towards the window to watch the rain fall.

OTHER TITLES IN THE SERIES

MAIGRET AND THE NAHOUR CASE
GEORGES SIMENON

'Maigret had often been called on to deal with individuals of this sort, who were equally at home in London, New York and Rome, who took planes the way other people took the Metro, who stayed in grand hotels . . . he had trouble suppressing feelings of irritation that might have been taken for jealousy.'

A professional gambler has been shot dead in his elegant Parisian home, and his enigmatic wife seems the most likely culprit – but Inspector Maigret suspects this notorious case is far more complicated than it appears.

Translated by Will Hobson

OTHER TITLES IN THE SERIES